Kundera
or
The Memory of Desire

Kundera
or
The Memory of Desire

Eva le Grand

translated by
Lin Burman

We acknowledge the support of the Canada Council for the Arts for our publishing program.

We acknowledge the financial support of the Government of Canada through the Book Publishing Industry Development Program for our publishing activities.

Canada

Canadian Cataloguing in Publication Data

Le Grand, Eva
   Kundera, or, The memory of desire

Translation of: Kundera, ou, La Mémoire du desir.
Includes bibliographical references and index.
ISBN 0-88920-327-X

1. Kundera, Milan—Criticism and interpretation. 2. Kitsch in literature. 3. Desire in literature. I. Burman, Lin, 1950- . II. Title. III. Title: Memory of desire.

PG5039.21.U6Z5513 1999   89148'6354   C99-931277-4

© 1999
Wilfrid Laurier University Press
Waterloo, Ontario N2L 3C5

Cover design by Leslie Macredie

Cover illustration by Milan Kundera

To my son Alexandre

[E]sthetics, as a discipline, might well be a science which does not examine works as such, but rather works as they speak to the reader or viewer: a sort of typology of discourses if you will.*   — Roland Barthes

[T]he essay . . . the modificatory test of itself in the game of truth rather than a modificatory appropriation of others.*
        — Michel Foucault

Table of Contents

Foreword

A Collaborative Reading

Here is an essay, the publication of which I consider significant, that examines Milan Kundera's novels in their entirety, up to the break marked by the novel *Slowness*, in which the change of language (Kundera wrote it directly in French) marks the clear beginning of a new phase. I am well aware that there already existed other comprehensive studies on the novel cycle begun by *The Joke*, at least one of which has been published; but the novelty and remarkable nature of Eva Le Grand's work (*that* is its significance) lies in the fact that it deals with Kundera exclusively as a novelist—and does not, as has been the case too often in the past, draw him into the domain of philosophy, or worse still, make him into a sort of "intellectual guide."[1] Is this a work of literary criticism, then? Yes, but in the broadest sense of the term, and one which distinguishes it from mere "news about literary current events" which have supplanted it more or less everywhere and especially in the press.[2] Literary criticism, in the opinion of Kundera himself, is an absolutely necessary genre, whose creators have in fact nothing to fear, quite the contrary. Insofar that it is a matter of pondering over a work (and not merely giving an account of it); grasping its newness and originality; entering into the complexity (quite diabolical in this case) of the composition and stylistic devices; being able to tie it into a global context (that of the "art of the novel" in general), the only thing likely to allow its value to be appreciated; and, above all, endeavouring to bring out the unperceived part of human experience, which every great novelist has the task of bringing about, and which, according to the now accepted formula, could not be brought about by means other than those specific to the novel. To say that Eva Le Grand fulfils the task, as Kundera has several times postulated (I am merely repeating his own suggestions here) is an understatement; it must also be specified that she does so with a quite exceptional breadth of vision and subtlety of analysis.

Notes to the Foreword are on p. 129.

The pitfalls, however, were many, and particularly, that of para-phrase, since the difficulty (as we know) in Kundera's case is that he is *also* the author of authoritative critical works, where he cannot fail to appear, among other things, as the best commentator of his own nov-els. This is where Eva Le Grand's work compels our admiration: rather than remain tied to the "first hand" commentary, and be satisfied with redistributing it (which would have been the easy way out), she has chosen instead to take side roads, to chart untrodden, seemingly meandering, paths between the themes and motifs to which Kundera's work beckons, to establish, within the seven novels she examines, all kinds of correlations, shortcuts and short circuits, and to reveal in them their hidden consistencies and hitherto unsuspected contrasts; she has done this, to the point of revealing a portrait of Kundera the novelist which one could certainly sense, and for which she now pro-vides an irrefutable foundation and conclusive proof: a portrait of one of the greatest and most comprehensive *demystifiers* of our time.

We still need to agree on the term "demystification," the pet theme of "ideological criticism" as practised in the sixties and seven-ties, a term which these days no longer seems to serve any purpose. It was most often used (even Roland Barthes could not always get away from it—this is in fact why he later resisted extending *Mythologies*) in the name of a higher truth, an arrogant interpretive system, a meta-language supposedly possessing power "in the first degree" over the language it analyzed (hence its all too frequent inquisitorial dimen-sion). With Kundera, as Eva Le Grand demonstrates very clearly, it is nothing of the sort: if indeed there is "demystification," it occurs through laughter rather than intimidation; it occurs without any appearance of "ultimate truth," without any thesis being put forward to circumscribe the many experiences explored; in short, without any sacrifice of that share of laughter, irony and ambiguity which has char-acterized *all* great novels since Rabelais and Cervantes.

The function of any genuine writer has never been to approve of the world. But it is clear, from following Eva Le Grand in her critical course, that Kundera is today probably one of those who takes this actualist negativity the furthest; the one, in any case, who casts the most penetrating, most disillusioned, and most amused eye on all modern mythologies, on all our alliances, beliefs, commonplaces and conformities. Hence the following random targets in his novels: the "idyllic" view of the world, which supposes an indestructible dream of harmony; ubiquitous kitsch—a category which Kundera extracts from the esthetic domain alone, and turns into an almost universal key to our behaviour (and which allows him to counter a very common prejudice and to bring out the continuity existing between the communist universe and that of democratic societies); lyrical illusion, in all its forms, but especially the one which relentlessly poeticizes the world and finds something like a ghostly paradise lost; the religion of childhood, and the blind devotion to modernity as such (by virtue of which Kundera belongs to the tradition of a novelist such as Gombrowicz); the promotion of feeling as a value , and the worship of love-passion—romantic foolishness generally perceived as "natural," unlike the lucid and dominating eroticism posited; the great age of libertinism; totalitarianism in everyday life ushered in by the rule of widespread indiscretion which in reaction brings about the need to re-evaluate shame as an attitude which is henceforth subversive; the way in which the triumph of spectacle (and its variant which Kundera terms "imagology") has now supplanted the reign of ideology and been internalized to the point where all and sundry are constantly induced to live as though they were "in the eye of the cameras"; right-thinking is also widespread, and especially the paradoxical conformity of revolt or indignation—fueled by what Nietzsche termed the "slave revolt in morality," which makes the trial today's most common intellectual activity; systematic hatred of art, masked by official veneration which has become an inoffensive social ritual; confusion in values, and particularly the tremendous loss of meaning brought about by the proliferation of "self-expression" (the tremendous increase in "graphomania") and the profusion of messages conveyed (this could, in fact, be the most characteristic trait of our age: the age in which the words "to communicate" have, little by little, imperceptibly, become an intransitive verb). In short, we see this world of ours *as it is*, a sort of unanimously accepted subdued barbarism which constitutes the very horizon of our lives.

The negativity of Kundera's writing, in the way it approaches all this, is extremely uncommon—if we compare it to that of other major contemporary novels. It proceeds neither by bursts of invective and curses (as in the work of Thomas Bernhard), nor by ridiculous hyperbole (as in the work of Juan Goytisolo), nor by the strange ruses of fiction whose function is to undermine our certainties (as in the work of Danilo Kis or Philip Roth), nor by the explosion of a sort of apocalyptic carnival (as in the work of Carlos Fuentes or Salman Rushdie), nor by presenting the alienation of our lives in the most irrational fictions (as in the work of Mario Vargas Llosa), nor by the constant and harrowing turning over of traumatic and destructive elements (as in the work of

Claude Simon), nor by great narrative parables (as in the work of Kenz-
aburô Oé), nor by a position of interpretive projection (as in the work
of Philippe Sollers). As Eva Le Grand demonstrates in the clearest pos-
sible manner, this negativity proceeds rather through a series of varia-
tions (whose pattern is explicitly musical) on concrete experiences,
"existential paradoxes"—those of characters (defined by Kundera as
"experimental selves") propelled into borderline situations, unleashed
in a whole game of ambiguities and misunderstandings, confronted
with indistinct and yet decisive "borders"; all this is simultaneously
(as Musil claimed) recounted and thought—but originates in playful,
suspended thought, which does not overload the experiences, and
above all does not ultimately involve any positivity: the game remains
open.

I have touched on the musical pattern at work in this writing—
and I have never read anything on the subject as illuminating as the
pages devoted by Eva Le Grand to Kundera's particular, inimitable way
of "musicalizing" the novel. We know that Mallarmé, at the end of the
last century, wrote a piece entitled "La musique dans les lettres" in
which he contended that poetry was able to to appropriate what had
been until then the prerogative of music. Well, it could very well be
that from now on it falls to the novel to carry out the same appropri-
ation[3] on condition that one sees clearly that what is thus absorbed
stems less from direct sound effects (as was the case for Mallarmé)
than from the composition itself, whether we are dealing with princi-
ples and processes of the "Grand Form" (following in the steps of
Proust, Broch and Faulkner) or contrary to what Kundera terms
"Chopin's strategy," that which destroys the rhetoric of "development"
by recourse to brief, condensed forms. Eva Le Grand offers an acutely
perceptive explanation of the way in which the traditional dramatic
progression is supplanted in Kundera's work by a mode of narra-
tive structuring through "themes and variations"; how the semi-
autonomous "plot threads" are woven together on various levels,
which assumes the literary equivalent of a veritable art of counter-
point; how the multiplicity of voices (and the voice of the narrator-
author, she maintains, is only one among many, with no higher
authority) creates a veritable polyphony, where the reader is "the only
one to attain the relativity and complexity of truth"; how the hetero-
geneity of the subjects and the enmeshing of stories are counter-
invested by a whole series of thematic links at a distance, which she
terms nicely a "parade of echoes," and which prevent their dispersal,
and guarantee the novels, even the most fragmented of them, their

underlying cohesion; how, above all, the same distant play of echoes and narrative counterpoints can be found between the different novels of the cycle under study: the fabulous unity of the cycle in question is revealed, over and above all the variations, in the analysis of the meta-composition (which Eva Le Grand, it seems to me, is the first to demonstrate with such precision). But probably the most novel aspect of all this lies in her way of never reducing these biases to the sole domain of form or technique—or better still—of suggesting that for Kundera, as for any genuine novelist, the meaning lies *in* the technique; establishing for example a union between the "donjuanesque journey" of certain characters and the art of variation which also aims, both to "make a pleasant change" and to explore reality in its endless diversity.

But there is one point, especially, on which Eva Le Grand's work compels unreserved recognition—and it concerns her approach to the sexual lucidity at work in Kundera's novels. I, for one, have never looked contemptuously upon those adolescents (I was the same, at their age) who, on discovering the vast terrain of the novel, immediately engage in a feverish search for the passages dealing with "it." Their actions would point rather to very sound intuition, which any subsequent higher education will set its sights on eradicating. Basically, everyone lies about sex—and if a little truth can permeate what is endlessly disguised or unrecognized by *all* discourse, it is paradoxically to novelists, at the very heart of fiction, that we are indebted. What Eva Le Grand demonstrates, more exactly, is that in Kundera's work, this particular subject is the scene of constant tension between two polarities, which endlessly disturb each other, and to which she attributes the two mythical names of Don Juan and Tristan: on one hand, there is the womanizing attitude within which one must make several distinctions (there is nothing in common, for example, between the "wolf" who racks up conquests indiscriminately and the "libertine" who, for his part, chooses, and sets his sights on, not "women" in general, but a collection of scrupulously dissociated singularities); on the other hand, there is behaviour which, to use Kundera's words, "has raised feelings to a category of value," and seeks only, through love-madness, love-passion, *possession*, a sort of exalted, "lyrical," idealized fusion in which all domination ends. And most of Kundera's characters, as she demonstrates, are torn between them—caught in an uncontrollable fluctuation between the two which proves to be the source, in a way, of the most extreme comedy.

I reread, not long ago, an eighteenth-century masterpiece of libertinism (I was going to say "French," but it would be a tautology), *Les Liaisons dangereuses*. In it we find, for example, the following maxim, from the pen of the marquise de Merteuil: "Love, whose praises we sing to you for being the cause of our pleasure, is at most nothing but an excuse for it"*; or this phrase of Valmont's: "Here you are in the country, which is as dull as sentiment and as sad as fidelity."* There is no need to dwell on it; we are now far removed from the insolence, from the complete absence of innocence, in fact from the magnificent sovereignty, of lucid pleasure, which is probably the human race's best invention of its history (although its splendour was brief, isolated, for the few), which was the only true freedom worth anything (all others, in fact, ensue), and which knew how to put "feeling" in its place. All this, then, was very quickly denied, denigrated, accused, fought, concealed, forgotten (it is what Hermann Broch, quoted by Eva Le Grand, termed the "conspiracy of monogamous puritanism against the Age of Enlightenment"). It is in fact that decline, which Kundera explores, right up to our own age, in which libertinism has become subjectively almost impossible, in which Tristan always ends up getting in the way of Don Juan, in which even the so-called "sexual liberation" has amounted to hardly more than the mask of a banal lyrical and idyllic vision (one more way of conforming, sapped by its sentimental underside, and stemming from a collective utopia into which none of the libertines of the chosen century would have been ridiculous enough to sink); and in which, I might add, the latest find of "monogamous puritanism," sexual pleasure, is henceforth enjoined to be automatically associated with illness and death, by a carefully sustained Pavlovian reflex.

Which were the great "figures" of the libertine journey? Essentially, there were four:[4] choice, where the libertine affirmed his freedom and his remarkable character; seduction, where the pleasure of conquest was tied to exercising a talent for strategy and claimed as such; the "fall" which involved other talents and another kind of savoir faire, and which constituted as much the stakes of the journey as its object; finally, the breakup, a clean one, with no sentimental hitches, which achieved domination. All the characters presented by Kundera (and the picture painted by Eva Le Grand is perfectly clear) always end up on one or the other of these figures—if not on all of them. It is as though all kitsch today had blighted such possibilities for good: even Sabina, in *The Unbearable Lightness of Being*, who comes closest to the libertine ideal (and is, in my opinion, the most endearing of Kundera's characters) experiences her successive breakups only as an instinctive, unmastered impulse, a metaphor for being wrenched away from the constantly renewed maternal sphere, insofar as she has never really liberated herself from it. Even something as private (and, according to Kundera, as revealing of each individual sexuality) as excitement is, as Eva Le Grand so brilliantly demonstrates, Kundera sets the scene of the worst misunderstandings, the worst insanities, in a series of situations whose intrinsic comic dimension nobody, with the possible exception here again of Philip Roth, has explored until now.

It remains for me to emphasize a vital point. Basically, the teaching of literature, as it is generally practised, hardly aims to do anything more than to render insipid or to eclipse the violence it carries. To put it bluntly, literature is not taught, people are taught to relieve it of everything in it which can threaten consensus, challenge idyllic notions of the world, upset conformity, and dissipate the illusions on which all social connections are based. Eva Le Grand, for her part, is a professor, that is to say she is assigned in principle to inscribe literature in a pedagogical framework—and yet, as this work shows brilliantly, nothing could be more alien to her than the current practice of rendering literature sterile. It is this, as much as her perfect knowledge of the slightest aspect of the work in question, and the exceptional complicity she obviously maintains with it, which for me constitutes the most important quality of her essay: nothing of Kundera's extraordinary insolence is erased; not even the most scatological motifs of his novels, which are certainly touched on here without the slightest vulgarity (one sometimes thinks of the elegant discourse of which Barthes was capable on particularly scabrous passages of Sade); her mastery of the power of dis-idealization of these motifs is complete. In fact, the two go hand in hand: there is no overall unifying thesis which would correspondingly diminish the complexity of Kundera's work (this, as we know, is the most common failing of standard academic works)—but neither is there anything of the conventional and implicit moralism which would aim to narrow its subversive range. So it is that a book such as this (where sometimes, even in the midst of the most subtle analyses, a hint of verve, liable to wreck the academic discourse, shows through) is closely akin to the pleasure to be had from reading Kundera's novels themselves: what he himself calls "the strange pleasure that comes of the certainty that there is no certainty," and which Eva Le Grand, for her part, terms, in a nice turn of phrase, "the novel's laughter in the face of the imposture of all absolutes." One cannot imagine in this respect a better incentive to read (or reread) Kundera than this essay: it expresses, in all its non-conformity, a pleasure which Eva Le Grand renders irresistibly contagious.

Guy Scarpetta
La Lauze, August 1995

Abbreviations

The abbreviations and references to Kundera's books are cited as follows:

AN: *The Art of the Novel*. Translated from the French by Linda Asher. New York: HarperCollins, 1993.

BLF: *The Book of Laughter and Forgetting*. Translated from the French by Aaron Asher. New York: HarperCollins, 1996.

FP: *The Farewell Party*. Translated from the French by Aaron Asher. New York: HarperCollins, 1998.

IMM: *Immortality*. Translated from the Czech by Peter Kussi. New York: HarperCollins, 1992

JM: *Jacques and His Master*. Translated from the French by Michael Henry Heim. New York: HarperCollins, 1985.

JOKE: *The Joke*. English translation fully revised by the author. New York: Harper Perennial, 1993.

LIFE: *Life Is Elsewhere*. Translated from the Czech by Peter Kussi. Toronto: Penguin, 1986.

LL: *Laughable Loves*.Translated from the Czech by Suzanne Rappaport. Toronto: Penguin, 1987.

SLO: *Slowness*. Translated from the French by Linda Asher. New York: HarperCollins, 1995.

TB: *Testaments Betrayed*. Translated from the French by Linda Asher. New York: HarperCollins, 1995.

ULB: *The Unbearable Lightness of Being*. Translated from the Czech by Michael Henry Heim. New York: HarperCollins, 1987.

Note: An asterisk (*) after a quotation indicates that the translation is by Lin Burman.

Introduction

Whereof one cannot speak, thereon one must remain silent
— Ludwig Wittgenstein, *Tractatus*

The essay before you must be understood in the original, in Montaigne's meaning of the term, that is, not as a philosophical or ideological study, but as a self-searching progression, as an open, critical reflection whose subject has not been exhausted. It is therefore not only out of modesty that I state from the outset that this essay does not in any way offer an exhaustive or definitive reading of the cycle of Kundera's seven novels, but rather the knowledge acquired during my many rereadings of his word, each one of which represented only one of many other possible readings, given that the artistic structure of Kundera's novels is so complex and literally inexhaustible. Kundera's works, those of one of the late twentieth century's greatest ironists and most relentless demystifiers of all absolutes, in fact teach us above all a fundamental "truth": the absolute relativity of all things human and, consequently, the incompleteness and relativity of all knowledge—that of humanity, of oneself and of every true work of art.

It was impossible for me to uncover in a single study all the formal and semantic aspects of the seven novels examined, all the more so since I was anxious to read them as a single text, which, in my opinion, is the only possible way to grasp the esthetic coherence of Kundera's art. Of course, there were times when, discouraged and faced with the devilish complexity of these constantly changing works, I almost yielded to the temptation to examine each of the seven novels in isolation. However, I knew that while this would certainly have made my task easier by leading me rapidly to the finale, it would, on the other hand, have made me miss my goal altogether. Awareness of this fact would repeatedly draw me back to the albeit well-trodden "paths" of his works, and I have, in the process, been handsomely rewarded throughout my years of critical reflection with a pleasure steadily renewed by new insights and discoveries.

The four chapters devoted in this book to Kundera's cycle of novels represent four studies which are different but complementary as regards their common effort to define, using various problematics as a springboard, the esthetic value of the whole. Whether I explore the function of kitsch in Kundera's work, the journey of the variations into the European novel's "well of the past," the functioning of its variation and polyphony, or the esthetic function of its many donjuanesque figures, I always aim to seize the moment in which the different echoes of his work contribute in unison to its esthetic value. For me, Kundera's novels are neither ideological nor historical, neither philosophical nor autobiographical, but novels which are profoundly polyphonic, polysemic and, especially (above all, perhaps), superbly playful, fictional. Kvetoslav Chvatik is quite right to refer to them, most aptly, as "pure novels." Furthermore, their formal and semantic structures are indissociable to the point where, when I explore, for example, the discontinuous and repetitive course of Kundera's Don Juans, I inevitably embark once more on the journey of his variations and vice versa. This example is only one among many other possible examples in a body of work in which the formal and narrative structures, imaginary selves and thematic developments coincide.

In fact, reading these works provides and excellent apprenticeship in the existential paradox, as their truths on all and sundry are so numerous, some simultaneously contradicting and complementing others, releasing Kundera's inimitable laughter from their reciprocal tension. Such a fictional vertigo where characters, themes, form and playful meditation come together, such a "crossroads of multiplicity," to use of Kundera's own definitions of the novel, has no need, as one can well imagine, of extratextual historical "reality" and "truth." Besides, the novelist firmly emphasizes the fact that his novels do not examine "reality," but existence; or to put it another way, they examine the world of possibilities, whether this is incarnated or not in his characters. For the novelist, it is above all a question of never ending the questioning of the as-yet-unexplored possibilities of human existence and of continuing to write and rewrite "to retain memory." Critics who examine this masterly work should therefore, *a fortiori,* keep their questioning open and continue the search for possible new ways of combining the mnesic "paths," both formal and semantic, of which it is composed. In fact, even the word "memory," in the title I have given to my essay, could have been written in the plural as well as in the negative mode—so true is it that everything (the meanings and values of the themes, situations, etc.) in this body of work is inter-changeable.

For Kundera, the novel represents above all an exploration of the possibilities of human existence through the characters, his imaginary selves. And yet, it is not the plot, but the thematics which constitute the unity of his work. It is moreover no coincidence that the problematics I examine in the first chapter are those of a theme, and what is more, the theme of kitsch. Kitsch is understood, as it is by the novelist, as a "categorical agreement with being," like the reduction of all plurality to a one-dimensional, idealized and false reality. In other words, kitsch in Kundera's work is precisely what the irony of his variational repetitions constantly subverts, diverts and deconstructs. Furthermore, since in Kundera's work kitsch is, in varying degrees, the most insidious "existential code" of all his characters, it represents for me the fundamental theme of all his work and the one whose development can be traced from the first to the last of his texts. Moreover, the theme of kitsch constitutes not only the basic element of existential questioning in Kundera's work, but also, if I may be allowed the metaphor, the centre of effort of all his other basic themes, especially time, love, memory, beauty and laughter. Be it ideological or imagological, I examine kitsch in its connection with the forgetting of being, in its insidiously seductive way of transforming the world into an "emotional plague," as Broch put it, as lyrical as it is narcissistic. But I explore especially the way in which Kundera's variation, in its numerous ironic strategies, eludes kitsch at the same time as it exposes it as a reductive representation of the world based on the denial of human time, so that even desire lives on as no more than a desire for eternity.

Through its numerous thematic variations, Kundera's variation, as may well be imagined, reveals a great deal more than the mere existential level of its characters. Beyond these, it constantly questions the very essence of European history, which is also examined as an existential situation. In order to do this, Kundera invites us on a journey inside the time of Europe and, in a masterly fusion of fiction and reflection, in so doing releases four echoes of the European novel, the "four appeals" which drive his own art of combination: the appeals of time, of play, of dream and of thought. In this way, by following the narrative, discursive and formal traces of the appeals of time and play throughout his work, I discover his "esthetic of the palimpsest," an esthetic which knowingly revives the "first period" of the history of the European novel (that of Rabelais, Cervantes, Sterne and Diderot) and, above all, its laughter. I then examine the appeals of dream and

thought which link Kundera's art to the great Central European novel-
ists of the beginning of the twentieth century, to Kafka, Musil, Broch
and Gombrowicz to name but a few. Here again, beyond the themes
privileged by his variational repetitions, it is once more a question of
man caught as an object in the trap of history. With superb irony, Kun-
dera contrasts a vast number of small episodes and stories (often of a
sexual or scatological nature) with the larger history, thereby revealing
the profoundly comical aspect of the latter. In this second excursion
through his work, I also summon the figure of Don Juan—that of
knowledge—because his "epic" adventure stands out against the dif-
ferentiating repetition of the variation and because their courses, erotic
for the character and scriptural for the novelist, unite in their ironic
opposition to the other repetition, the imitative and obliterating repeti-
tion of kitsch.

"Variation-novel or crossroads," the second chapter in the section
devoted to the esthetic qualities of Kundera's variation (and the third
in the essay as a whole) attempts more specifically to examine the for-
mal possibilities explored by the novelist in his simultaneously playful
and cognitive synthesis of variation and polyphony. What is more, his
art of composition combines three basic principles—the art of ellipsis,
the art of counterpoint at that of the specifically novelistic essay—
which have been commented on at length by Kundera himself in his
critical writing as well as by the narrator of his fictional works, and
which his readers cannot therefore help but be familiar. However, while
remaining attentive to the author's comments on the form of his nov-
els, I have continually tried to trace the connections between his com-
positional bias of the theme with variations and his semantic and
existential exploration. The conception of the character of a novel, the
particular status of Kundera's narrator within the discursive poly-
phony as well as, it goes without saying, the strictly formal interplay
of variation are examined here with the aim of grasping the core of the
essentially phenomenological mode of Kundera's esthetic, a mode
which underscores even further the indissociability of form and con-
tent in his work. I then address the various aspects of the essential
point, and undoubtedly the most innovative, in Kundera's art of com-
position: his interplay with the plot. For not only does this interplay
change from one novel to the next, bestowing on his work an excep-
tionally multiform construction, but in addition, Kundera, of all the
novelists of this century, best addresses in my view both the semantic
paradox and that of the form of the novel, inasmuch as he pushes fur-
thest the dislocation, the suppression of the plot even (I am thinking

especially of *Immortality* but also of *Slowness*) although without ever giving up his obvious desire to tell stories, his pleasure in storytelling!

Although, in my examination of the formal and semantic aspects of the esthetic quality of Kundera's variation, I have never entirely lost sight either of kitsch with its mimetic and reductive repetitions, or of the differentiating repetitions of his Don Juans, I turn exclusively, in the last chapter devoted to the cycle of novels, to the existential possibilities of love which he explores throughout his work as a whole. However, "Don Juan's final glance or the memory of desire,"the title of the last part of the essay, in no way attempts to make an inventory of the countless situations of love and desire which, in Kundera's work, constitute, practically without exception, the fundamental existential history of the characters. Quite the contrary, I take only a few of his exploratory paths of love, in search of Europe's inner time, in search of a secret border which separates both the memory of forgetting and the novel of life, and, above all, Tristan's amorous feeling of a donjuan-esque desire. In my reading, the Don Juan figure viewed in his double textual journey (both scriptural and erotic) clearly reveals desire as the mostly exacerbated and ambiguous form of human time and, consequently, as being all the illusions of our supposed free will in love in general and in our era's love of "terminal paradoxes" in particular. Kundera's ironic genius here reaches its height, as he succeeds in maintaining the historical continuity of love through Don Juan, that figure of discontinuity par excellence. In exploring the paradox between an asentimental eroticism and sentimental love (as kitsch and as lyrical as one could wish), he shows Don Juan and Tristan no longer in conflict, as did Denis de Rougemont, but in a "double exposure" which reveals desire caught in the trap of a double repetition, caught up between the irony of his journey of donjuanesque knowledge and nostalgia for the circular repetition of an idyllic paradise lost. In his phenomenological examination of the theme of love, in exploring the border zone between eroticism and licit sexuality, between irony and nostalgia, Kundera succeeds brilliantly in revealing the inadmissible: all the essentially comical elements concealed in human sexuality! Here, even the word "love" is explored through a multiplicity of meanings, which allows me the run the entire gamut of amorous situations from "love-emotion" (ridiculously kitsch in its illusory desire for eternity) to the lucidity of finiteness of "love-relation." In *Immortality,* the desire of the last Don Juan of the novelistic score in seven movements only survives, at the end of its journey, in the form of a few souvenir-images which are already more the product of forgetting desire itself than of its erotic memory. Of the memory of desire there only remains in fact, as a sign of the termination of the double donjuanesque journey, a desire for memory—borne by a nostalgic gaze back to Europe's past, to its "erotic dream."

I rejected the idea of "concluding" my essay with an epilogue on my own thoughts concerning Kundera's septenary cycle and have opted to conclude with a fresh look at the "erotic dream" of Europe's past and thereby respect the intrinsically open nature of Kundera's work. Although the publication of *Slowness* in many respects marks a break with the cycle of seven novels, it has provided me with an unexpected opportunity to do this. In Kundera's first novel written in French, the erotic moment at the end of the twentieth century is no longer anything but a pretence and one which in the gaze that the narrator-novelist turns to the libertine society of the eighteenth century, is no longer anything more than a pale and extremely comical reflection.

Part One

Kitsch and the Desire for Eternity

Before we are forgotten, we will be turned into kitsch. Kitsch is the stopover between being and oblivion.

— Milan Kundera, *The Unbearable Lightness of Being*

Who am I ? . . . You are the one in memory, You are the other in forgetting.*   — Carlos Fuentes, *Terra Nostra*

It is impossible to define all aspects of kitsch, as it represents the most multiform category of the esthetic and sociological, as well as the philosophical and cultural fields. Broch once said that every work of art contains its "drop of kitsch" and, in Adorno's view, it was futile to try and draw a line between esthetically pleasing fiction and sentimental plagiarizing with which kitsch invests it. It is also impossible to identify kitsch with bad taste, as do certain critics, even today. Adopting such a cliché would amount to forgetting that while the artistic modernism of this century evolved largely as a reaction to kitsch, the concept and status of kitsch have since then gone through several axiological metamorphoses.[1]

The most significant change in the artistic use of kitsch belongs however to the art of the novel which, by an ironic integration of various paradigms of kitsch into its structural interplay, exposes it as the most insidious expression of our semantic pretences and impostures, indeed of our most deep-seated anthropological illusions. Of all the production of contemporary novels with which I am familiar, it is Kundera's variations which, in their dually playful and cognitive journey, point to his novels as the example par excellence of such critical integration. Even if the term kitsch appears only in *The Unbearable Lightness of Being*, Kundera's work, from the first to the last of his texts, is filled with its multiform representation through the attitudes of his characters.

Notes to Part One are on pp. 129-30.

The Referential Illusion

To relate the idea of kitsch solely to objects, a particular style or a question of taste, necessarily erases its philosophical and anthropological dimension. It happens to be Kundera who has reminded us that kitsch is an existential category and that it must be understood above all as an attitude of the *Kitschmensch*, as an expression of the fascinating and ineradicable human faculty of substituting dreams of a better world (paradise lost as bright future) for reality, in short, of misrepresenting what is real as an idyllic and ecstatic vision of the world to which we sacrifice without scruple all ethical and critical awareness.

Kitsch thus offers us emotional (phantasmic) satisfaction of the subject, and this can then be defined, as Kundera does after the manner of Broch, as the " need (of kitsch-man) to look at himself in the mirror of beautifying lies and recognize himself with emotional satisfaction" or as "the translation of the stupidity of received ideas into the language of beauty and emotion."[*2] For Kundera, this sense of the word kitsch makes of it a phenomenon which is consubstantial with a being, who, far from being tied to a given historical period, becomes an esthetic expression of all "categorical agreement with being,"[3] this agreement implying a blind, unconditional and uncritical adherence to the representation of a world without conflicts (private or collective) as we would wish it or as various ideologies or imagologies strive to make it appear.

If we compare the kitsch attitude as represented by Kundera with the two basic anthropological attitudes, on one hand with a representation whose referent is present and immediate and, on the other, with a representation through objectivation[4] whose referent is an image or an idea, kitsch obviously bears certain similarities with the latter. It can, however, be distinguished from the collection of attitudes as a whole by objectivation through its strict adherence to the domain of feeling and emotion. The very knowledge of the world becomes contaminated, all the more so because it does not rest on a real-life feeling, but on an imitation of feeling. The text of *Immortality* contains a wealth of examples of such sentimentalist imitations or attitudes; Laura and Bettina constitute without a doubt the most perfect representations of this. Experiencing feelings shall I say "by proxy," their emotion rests on a representation to the nth power, on an emotion of the emotion or on the emotion before the image of the emotion. This is precisely what Kundera expresses through his metaphor of the second tear in *The Unbearable Lightness of Being*:

> Kitsch causes two tears to flow in quick succession. The first tear says: How nice to see children running on the grass! The second tear says: How nice to be moved, together with all mankind, by children running on the grass! It is the second tear that makes kitsch kitsch. The brotherhood of man on earth will be possible only on a base of kitsch. (ULB, p. 251)

Lyrical Ecstasy

Kundera's metaphor of the second tear shows clearly how kitsch results in an ecstatic and illusory vision of the world which sacrifices all reflection for the benefit of the sole glorification of feeling. Nietzsche declared a long time ago that, in order to act, man needs to cover his eyes with a blindfold of illusions. Kundera's work offers innumerable paths which explore such emotions, the principal source of lyricism and sentimentalism, especially in the face of love and death. The best example of this remains the poet Jaromil in *Life Is Elsewhere,* for whom the representation of death refers merely to a picture devoid of its real dimension, to a metaphysical absolute which snaps its fingers at the materiality of a body which has become a corpse. Jaromil's affairs are not much different, since his feeling of love draws its greatness from the absolute image of death, dismissing a priori any relativity whose reality might risk tainting it. For her part, Bettina von Arnim in *Immortality* represents the most accomplished feminine artisan of a love emotion, with the result that, "true love" which she decides to feel for Goethe, has a great deal more to do with the lyrical ecstasy of her own narcissistic self (with her desire for immortality) than with love for a concrete man.

Jaromil or Bettina, but also Laura, Paul, Brigitte and many others, experience love's intense emotions in dreams and compensatory phantasms, finding the reality of conflict nothing but disappointing.[5] In fact, unlike Tomas, Sabina, Agnes or Goethe, Jaromil and Bettina do not know (do not want to know!) that an extreme emotion reduces the image of the world in its own manner, by opening up the way to sentimental ecstasy and to the reassuring "kingdom of the heart" where kitsch and forgetting operate in unison.

Double Exposure

In order to counter the reductive work orchestrated by kitsch, Kundera subjects his themes and characters to a double semantic exposure which brings out simultaneously two theoretically incompatible worlds, letting them be seen in their surprising proximity. In this case, it allows him to expose, behind the rosy colours of kitsch representation, the multicoloured world of an erased reality and vice versa. Through the rent in the socialist-realist canvasses which Sabina is forced to execute at the Academy of Fine Arts in Prague, quite a different world shows through: "behind the backdrop's cracked canvas," the double exposure reveals the "intelligible lie" of appearances to give us a glimpse of what is hidden behind . . . Moreover, Sabina's cycle of canvasses is entitled *Behind the Scenes*. Seeing through the backdrops in order to expose what is hidden behind the facades, behind the masks of beauty through which kitsch conceals the conflictual reality, becomes the metaphor which links Sabina's art to the art of Kundera's variation: they both see through the insidious intrusion of the mendacious reality between self and the world or, to put it in the words of the narrator of *Immortality,* between the self and the image of the self.

The ironic interplay with kitsch which Kundera's variations put in place succeeds in bringing out the vague totalitarian impulses concealed in any emotional seductiveness of kitsch by depriving us, to begin with, of our power to differentiate between the real and the imaginary or, to give the most semantically marked example of this in Kundera's work, between love-relation and love-emotion.

Kundera's characters possess, in varying degrees, their "drop of kitsch," the unconscious guide of their intrigues and, above all, of their relation to time. For some, kitsch even becomes the sole existential code, both the most secret and the most underhand. At the risk of being somewhat heretical, I submit that any representation of an idealized, eternal and utopian human temporality can only assert itself in art as kitsch, in the form of a desire for eternity which erases chronology and even, in so doing, death. After all, is not happiness, as *The Unbearable Lightness of Being* suggests, the nostalgic desire to repeat time which, however, in our lifetimes, never returns? If art, as Adorno claimed, is "the promise of happiness which is broken," kitsch could well be defined as the promise of happiness which is compensatory but with pretensions to truth. Happiness which offers us, in the end, only a parody of the catharsis of which Adorno speaks, or, to put it Broch's way, a book of imitative recipes. Broch once wrote that the modern novel makes a heroic attempt to stem the tide of kitsch, but it will end up being overwhelmed by it, and Kundera took up this statement in his acceptance speech with the quintessentially Brochian title "God's Laughter" when he was awarded the Jerusalem Prize in 1985. In it he examines the seductiveness of kitsch which has become the daily imperative of the age of mass media where "to be modern means a strenuous effort to be up-to-date, to conform, to conform even more thoroughly than the most conformist of all." To be modern therefore means a strenuous effort to resemble one's own image, a crucial theme in *Life Is Elsewhere* as well as in *Immortality*, the ultimate vision of our civilization which is already engulfed, like Atlantis, in ubiquitous visual and acoustic kitsch.

Kitsch as a "Categorical Agreement with Being"

The Unbearable Lightness of Being rests mainly on a multiplicity of ways of exploring the conspicuous theme of kitsch which moreover, in the book, becomes the main axis of the architectonics of the whole of part six. Kundera's meditation conceives of kitsch as the esthetic expression of all categorical agreement with being, clearly confirming its ontological meaning by the novelist.

Furthermore, Kundera uncovers, in the most provocative way, the origin of this agreement in the first chapter of Genesis, in the sacrosanct imperative which links love to procreation, to an infinite multiplication of God's "good" creation. The refusal of a great many of his characters, among them Jacques, Jakub, Tomas, Sabina or Rubens, to procreate, must be considered in the light of this paradox. Jakub in *The Farewell Party*, for example, dreams of separating love from procreation while his friend, the famous doctor Skreta, is fulfilling the old eugenic dream of procreation without love, since the numerous children engendered by his own sperm bear a horrifying resemblance to one single image, that of God-Skreta . . .

But beyond all these implications of a private nature, the first categorical agreement with being stands out, declares the narrator, against all Western beliefs, be they religious or secular. Political parties, like religious sects, agree on the same archetypal representation. Differences among various groups are merely a question of degree and symbol: march forward, fist raised, the name of the president of the United States, index finger pointed, and so on. It is as though, from this point of view, but from this point of view only, the symbols of the hammer and sickle, of Christ on the cross, or the swastika refer to the same archetypal image, all expressing the same agreement with greatest number, the same appeal to the solidarity of the herd. The irony with which Kundera describes the "Grand March" of the European and American left on the Cambodian border, represents both the darkest and the most grotesque aspect of political kitsch.

God, Paradise and Shit

To circumvent and subvert the apodictic seriousness of theological discourses, Kundera transports his novelistic meditation on the first categorical agreement with being to territory tailor-made for man, by confronting it with its intrinsic "impurity." Like all good fun-loving practical jokers, and Devil's advocates, he questions the motto-cliché according to which God created people in his image, so that they should recognize themselves in the image of divine creation with unfailing satisfaction. Now there is, as you might say, a small problem: either humanity was created in the image of God who therefore also possesses intestines, or God does not have any and, in that case, he becomes responsible for humanity's defecatory ignominy. Consequently, kitsch's metaphor par excellence becomes the "absolute denial of shit" as shit evacuates everything which makes humanity different from the image of a God wreathed in purity. Far from being a provocative embellishment or a mere indulgence of the novelist, the scatological element in Kundera's work becomes one of the main factors of irony and laughter, through this, a structurally necessary counterpoint to the idyllic representation of all the agreements (ideological and imagological) with being.

The irony of Kundera's variations on kitsch reveals itself to its full subversive extent especially when it counterposes the scatological with death, particularly death in war, by bringing out its shamefully comical side. The death of Iakov, Stalin's son, which opens part six of the novel, here becomes the only metaphysical death in the carnage of the Second World War precisely insofar as Iakov laid down his life "for shit,"both literally and figuratively. Forced to clean out the latrines in the prison camp and unable to tolerate the "vertiginous proximity" of shit and the image of Stalin-God, his all-powerful father, Iakov dies on the electrified barbed-wire fence surrounding the camp.

Concerning Excitement

Shit, a more difficult theological problem than evil, also acquires its metaphysical title in the link which the variations establish between it and excitement, the very basis of eroticism in Kundera's work. A playful transcription of Johannes Scotus Erigenus' ninth-century theological thought offers an ironic meditation on the "theodicy of shit" placed in relation to the very idea of paradise. Even if Erigenus acknowledged coitus between Adam and Eve in paradise, he associated it with the image of an all powerful Adam, able to raise his member without excitement—therefore without devilish female temptation, as one raises an arm or a leg. A strange kind of "erotic paradise" in short (for what is eroticism without excitement?). The stuff of dreams for the men of today and of liberation for Eve from her tiresome and everlasting plans for seduction.

What happens to a man for him to be deprived of such power? The discovery of excitement, linked as it happens, to that of filth. In fact, the scatological variations, especially those in part six of *The Unbearable Lightness of Being*, state through the negative that "the objection to shit is a metaphysical one. The daily defecation session is daily proof of the unacceptability of Creation," hence its denial by all beliefs, religious or secular. No one is entirely safe from the lyrical nostalgia of that lost purity, not even Kundera's Don Juans. I am thinking of Jan in *The Book of Laughter and Forgetting* who dreams of finding the island of Daphnis and Chloe who were acquainted with desire without being acquainted with sexuality. But I am thinking especially of Tomas, a Don Juan transformed into Tristan by his Tereza, and who starts to dream of being able to have an erection at the sight of a swallow.

The share of kitsch in some character or other in Kundera's work can be measured according to their acceptance or refusal of shit and excitement. As Scarpetta suggests with regard to *The Unbearable Lightness of Being*, there are those who reject shit by becoming entangled in their own lyrical illusions (Tereza), those who accept it by denying all idea of sin (Tereza's mother) and those whose intermediate and libertine attitude accepts shit, sin and arousal all at once, of which the eroticism between Sabina and Tomas becomes an explicit example.[6]

The Danger of Metaphors

If all ideologies, religious or secular, hinge on the categorical agreement with being, it follows that kitsch becomes their common esthetic ideal. The fact remains that Kundera distinguishes between as many types of kitsch as beliefs. Although these beliefs share the same identificatory agreement with being, they nonetheless differ one from the other by virtue of the metaphor which expresses that being. What is being: "But what is the basis of being? God? Mankind? Struggle? Love? Man? Woman? Since opinions vary, there are various kitsches:

Catholic, Protestant, Jewish, Communist, Fascist, democratic, feminist, European, American, national, international" (ULB, pp. 256-57), the list is apparently as long as that of archetypal images, metaphors by which, unknown to us, we so often let ourselves be trapped.

Let us consider love born of a metaphor, what is more, a biblical one (that of a child found in a basket daubed with pitch), that of Tomas for Tereza. But let us also consider Bettina's "divine love" for Goethe which is a product of her desire for immortality and not of love for a concrete man. One can hardly spare Agnes, who suddenly realizes that her life with Paul is solely a matter of her will to love and not love, similar in this respect to Kamila in *The Farewell Party* whose love for Klima stems solely from the idea of her own jealousy.

Similarly with the "collective" lovers. From Helena Zemanek to Madame Rafael and her students, from Eluard to the angel-children of Tamina's island, from Edwige's edenic dream to Franz of the "Grand March," they all obey, in their feelings, loves and actions, the seductiveness exerted by the reassuring metaphors of an idyll for all: circle, dance, singing, rhythmic march become in Kundera's work so many sources of an idyllic collective seduction, so many beautiful metaphors which make human time stand still by substituting it for a state of eternal happiness, an esthetic ecstasy kept alive in short by a repetition of sameness. Whether it calls itself lyrical or romantic, the kitsch attitude is characterized by its particular relationship to existential time, by the transformation of its disquieting complexity into a superb mirage of timelessness. Was Nietzsche thinking of kitsch when he wrote that humanity's long blindness hinges on its esthetic taste, on its obstinate stubbornness in demanding from truth a picturesque effect?[7]

Logic of the Mirror

The reduction of life's disorder to the life of magical order of lyrical uniforms becomes the main objective of the variations in *Life Is Elsewhere*.[8] For Jaromil, life with its parade of disagreements has gone elsewhere, leaving room for the rhymed and rhythmic harmonies of a poetry forgetful of itself, no longer reflecting anything but the poet's narcissistic image of the self with his compensatory universe where he reigns as the all-powerful God-creator. He certainly never suspects that he is nothing more than a manipulated and laughable God. Such is lyrical genius: his poems become so many fictitious affirmations and objectivations of himself and reality and, hence, so many tautological illusions. Such logic pushes the poet towards a schizoid dissociation between being and seeming, thereby freeing him from the weight of all responsibility in the face of his own acts and, consequently, from all guilt: the one responsible for the denunciation and imprisonment of his red-headed girlfriend is therefore not Jaromil himself, but (small comfort!) the image of Jaromil in love with the absolutes of love and the revolution, absolutes in the name of which he can betray with impunity both love and revolution. The reader is no longer surprised, for he has long known that the "houses of mirrors"or any other lyrical attitude (both private and collective) hardly hesitate to sacrifice a concrete person (millions of individuals, even!) in the name of abstract ideals and metaphors.

Through Jaromil's lyrical poetry transformed into the main paradigm of kitsch in *Life Is Elsewhere*, Kundera expresses his sharpest criticism of the manipulation of poetic language. Not a criticism of all poetry as a few hurried readers believe, any more than a criticism of a bad poet. One has only to read Jaromil's very first free verse to be convinced of his talent. What is more, the many historical reminders which speak of other lyrical poets (Lermontov, Rimbaud, Baudelaire, Shelley, Wolker, etc.) also caught in the trap both of their era and their mama, masterfully reduce Jaromil's lyrical attitude of which they become so many variations. Through such counterpoints which draw on the past of European culture, the novel makes the brilliant suggestion that all poetry carries within it the seed of possibility of belonging, in any historical context, to the kitsch vision. Categorical agreement with all revolutionary ideology demands of poetry that its rhythm be in harmony with the cadence of its march, with the heartbeat of the crowd. Establishing emotion as the absolute value of his poetry, as the unique value of its Stalinist age, Jaromil withdraws irremediably into compensatory language whose idealization, both emotional and semantic, signals its imposture.

The Making of a Hero

We learn, however, in the very first pages of the novel, that Jaromil was predestined to agreement with the being of poetry before he even came into the world. Mama deifies her unborn poet to the point of wishing to erase all trace of the biological father in order to model her future hero on the God Apollo, god of the Muses, but above all, of rhythm. What is more, his statuette is enthroned in a pathetic pose in the middle of the marital bedroom and Jaromil narrowly escaped being named Apollo—"he who has no human father." Poor poet, he has not even been able to choose his own metaphor!

From before his birth to Jaromil's last breath, the indefatigable mama weaves the reassuring prison of poetry around him. Seeking out traces of rhyme, even in his most banal child's expressions, she teaches him, along with speech, the "magic power" of rhythmic forms whose perfection makes us forget their content. In vain, Jaromil's father tries to register such idyllic "divine harmony" by hanging his stinking socks heroically on the fetish statuette of Apollo. In vain too, his grandfather tries naively to inculcate Jaromil with something of his own distrustful laughter in the face of all lyrical purity by teaching him, behind mother's back of course, funny and thoroughly stupid little rhymes.

From Disappointed Narcissus to Paper Don Juan

In this way, from his earliest childhood, Jaromil learns to talk not to communicate with others, but to seek in their expression a reflection of his beautiful prefabricated image, the reflection of an admiring agreement with his lyrical self. Alas, it so happens that, outside the maternal sphere, the image which some reflect back to Jaromil shatters any tautological illusion. The lady exasperated by the insipid logorrhea of young Jaromil who, wishing to be seen by everybody as "a child uttering significant words" (LIFE, p. 18) literally makes a spectacle of himself before a packed waiting room in the episode at the dentist's, the sniggering of his schoolmates as well as that of the artists who, unlike Jaromil, refuse to identify themselves with the esthetic imperative of socialist realism, all provide examples of this.

Where can Jaromil seek restorative images in the face of such narcissistic wounds? He does not even find them in the reflection of his own face which, as the patient but ever disappointed Narcissus, he observes at length in the mirror, searching for signs of nascent virility. For what the mirror reflects back to him is a feminine and angelic face, one which bears a hopeless resemblance to mama's. He has nothing but poetry, the sole remaining possibility of at last creating for himself a portrait of a virile man and of forgetting his immature self.

In the "house of mirrors" of his poetry, Jaromil thus abandons for ever the disquieting arrhythmia of his first verses (which would scarcely have been given space in the newspapers of the time) for the benefit of rhyming verse. In this way he can please everyone: mama, his red-headed girlfriend, the revolution, the Party and . . . the cops. Love, poetry and revolution belong henceforth to the same movement with the virilely revolutionary rhythm and the revolutionarily virile rhythm: " 'The more I make love, the more I want to make revolution—the more I make revolution the more I want to make love,' someone had written on a wall at the Sorbonne and Jaromil entered the red-headed girl for the second time" (LIFE, p. 181). Narcissus finally becomes Don Juan and little does he care that the image is only a paper image. . . .

Rhythm as a Metaphor of Total Order

Kundera's ironic genius, in the novel that was to have been called *The Lyric Age*, was able to make rhythm into the vital expression of all existential agreements. In his playful meditation, rhythm becomes for the narrator the main paradigm of kitsch: poetic rhythm agrees with the rhythm of the heart and body; individual biological rhythm, with the urges of the collective body. Rhyme and rhythm, we can well imagine, do not question but merely affirm, thereby becoming "the most brutal means of agreement with being." The historical parallels drawn between Jaromil and certain European poets all mark out rhyme and rhythm as being so many conditions of possibility of kitsch in any heightened form of lyricism.

Rhythm manages to render seductive all that is impure in human existence, to give even death a semantic facelift: "An amorphous world becomes at once orderly, lucid, clear, and beautiful when squeezed into regular meters. If a woman weary of breath has gone to her death, dying becomes harmoniously integrated into the cosmic order" (LIFE, p. 193). Rhythm (poetic in *Life Is Elsewhere*, musical in *The Book of Laughter and Forgetting*) possesses remarkable powers of semantic manipulation of both the vision of the world and the implicit values of language. Jaromil's socialist-realist poetry remains the best example. But his esthetic feeling reaches its height when he finds satisfaction in an act, by denouncing his girlfriend's brother to the police, a deed which allows the poet to enter into the total order of the world.

Moreover even Xavier, Jaromil's both imaginary and inaccessible alter ego, betrays the world of order which the poet establishes. Jaromil will never understand the betrayal. Born of the only attempt by the poet at a novel (no doubt just imagined by him as the narrator suggests), Xavier becomes another figure of the donjuanesque pursuit which characterizes Kundera's variations. He is a sort of imaginary incarnation of poetic relativity which, Jaromil, it so happens, betrays in the name of all lyrical absolutes. Xavier, linked to the metaphor of betrayal, can only flee, from one dream to another, the absolute order which Jaromil maintains, until his death, in his poetry.

Concerning an "Absolutely Modern" Realism

Rimbaud's imperative to be absolutely modern, transformed into Jaromil's central cliché-motto, in fact pervades all Kundera's work; in it, it reveals polyphonic and polysemic reality being reduced to a sham whose socialist-realist esthetic becomes the most blatant example. The Moravian popular songs referred to in *The Joke* are in their own way evidence of this. Their working-class code is rewritten according to the same imperative, an obliterative rewriting if ever there was, since only an impoverished form of its original functions is allowed to remain. These popular songs in it are "purged. . . . of all biblical motifs, even though it was precisely on these motifs that the imagery of the old nuptial speeches was based" (JOKE, p. 47). The "communist baptism" in *The Joke*, the nursery rhymes of the angel-children in *The Book of Laughter and Forgetting*, the radio interviews in *Immortality* and many other examples provide further evidence of the same reductive process.

In fact, Kundera's novels demonstrate in a variety of ways how kitsch implements structural simplification in art, how it reduces the primary meaning of a work to the benefit of a fixed and prefabricated meaning. Such a process, a semantic and structural imposture, insidiously shifts an artistic text into another context in which the structure loses its original characteristics of homogeneity and necessity while the "message" (the image) continues to present itself as an original work, capable of stimulating a new and original experience.[9] This is how kitsch goes about, in the most efficient way possible, its insidious task of forgetting. After all, Rimbaud's famous saying has also been transformed into a kitsch imperative through such a shift, and, finds itself in a context which, as Agnes in *Immortality* discovers, no longer has anything much in common with the poet of nature and paths that Rimbaud was.

Similar in this respect to Agnes rereading Rimbaud, Ludvik, listening to the "Ride of the Moravian Kings," also discovers the beauty of a forgotten reality: beyond the acoustic kitsch pouring out of the ubiquitous loudspeakers, he starts, by reinventing it, to hear the forgotten message of a veiled and mute king. He seizes the strange appeal of the past to restore to it a little of its initial meaning and its polyphony, something which a Jaromil, as the lyric bard of a glorious future, cannot do.

Thanks to his multiform variations on lyricism and kitsch, Kundera manages to invest his work with a powerful criticism of the age of democratized communication which in fact all too often conceals a reality in which seductiveness, narcissism and deafness go hand in hand with incommunicability. *Immortality*, whose variations transform ideological lyricism into imagological lyricism, offers the most terrifying portrayal of such deafness which has become total: beneath the grimace of an inevitable and ubiquitous (democracy oblige!) kitsch-laugh, no one hears anyone any more, for sounds and voices become inaudible here in the clamour of acoustic kitsch.

Novels, Kitsch and Beauty

Exploring the border between the epic and lyrical visions of Kundera's characters also allows us to define the basic difference between two types of beauty and knowledge: on one hand, there is the beauty generated by the essentially ironic and heterogeneous strategies of the novel, and on the other, that which stems from the positive and reductive strategies of kitsch. In order to grasp the difference, I follow the scattered paths of the very theme of beauty which crisscross Kundera's seven opuses. Mine is not a question of putting the markers of a concept in place, but more of discovering the novel's dramatization of the idea itself of the esthetic conflict between the novel and kitsch.

As an esthetic expression of the narcissistic need to gaze at one-self in objects and to regard as beautiful only that which reflects our image back to us,[10] kitsch is given to denying all heterogeneous knowledge and therefore all ambivalence. This does not in any way mean that Kundera, in his meditations on kitsch, confines it in abstract cognitive discourse, quite the contrary. "I do not wish to practise philosophy in the manner of a philosopher but in the manner of a novelist," he tells us, thereby clearly showing that his novels do not wish to define kitsch, but rather to suggest that if kitsch proliferates in all areas of this age of mass media, the art of the novel is duty bound to integrate it into its structure as one of its building materials in order to be able to pursue its questioning of all the possibilities of existence of which kitsch is henceforth a part. It is in fact a question of subverting and thwarting the seductive function exercised by kitsch to the benefit of an ironic distance appropriate for the novel. The novel thereby preserves the esthetic ambition of a sum of knowledge, and in so doing is able, despite the presence of kitsch, to create its own beauty.

In order to offer a utopian and ahistorical representation of the world, in short, an idyll from which everything dulling its celestial colours is eliminated, kitsch likes to feed off abstract ideals and feelings and sets them up as absolute values. Within such logic, it can only show illness, desire, the body or death under a " mask of beauty" to use one of the terms with which *The Unbearable Lightness of Being* refers to kitsch. It is through such esthetic and emotional idealization of what is real, especially when it prettifies deaths, wars, massacres, denunciations, executions or imprisonments, that kitsch becomes totalitarian: because purity, youth and beauty, in the name of which so many bloody crimes have been committed with smiles and songs on peoples' lips, come to be regarded as sacred. It is thanks precisely to the ironic integration of such representations that Kundera's novels point to the semantic and esthetic deception of kitsch as one of the greatest dangers of this century.

Broch once stated that since the Romantic movement, beauty in art is becoming a kitsch goddess, a vision which, since then, has undergone little change: whether we call it an esthetic lie (Eco), an esthetic of self-delusion (Calinescu) or of simulation (Baudrillard), kitsch, contrary to the knowledge of the novel, does not create its own beauty, since all its appeal remains parasitic to its referent, which, as I have said, is only an illusion. In other words, the appeal of kitsch in no way lies in a vision, but in an illusion of beauty.

If the appeal of kitsch stems from an order which is both emotional and esthetic, one must question the difference between its effects of knowledge and those produced act simultaneously by the novel. If the novel's vision of existence explores the particular through each of the characters, the kitsch representation on the other hand at once affirms the universality of each of its elements, which makes them reassuring emotionally. Kitsch therefore enriches neither our associations nor our relationship with the subject represented, any more than it exploits the artistic possibilities of structural elaboration.[11] Unlike kitsch, the modern novel does it almost programmatically. By using a code familiar to the receiver (cliché, stereotypes, hackneyed phrases or received ideas), the kitsch message prompts only an emotional response. Alternatively, a poetic message (non-kitsch), to take up Umberto Eco's distinction, is characterized by a fundamental ambiguity, allowing it to restore an interpretive tension in which emotion and critical knowledge.

To such questioning of the double register of knowledge, Kundera replies in the manner of a novelist. "What is esthetic pleasure?" he wonders. For him, such pleasure lies above all in the new light shed on something which has never before been said, shown or seen. The pleasure which *Madame Bovary*, for example, still brings us today stems in his view from the surprise of discovering that which we are not in a position to see in our daily lives:

> We have all met a Madame Bovary in one situation or another, and yet failed to recognize her. Flaubert unmasked the mechanisms of sentimentality, of illusions. He showed us the cruelty of and the aggressiveness of lyrical sentimentality. This is what I consider the knowledge of the novel. The author unveils a realm of reality that has not yet been revealed. This unveiling causes surprise and the surprise esthetic pleasure or, in other words, a sensation of beauty. On the other hand, there exists yet another beauty: beauty outside knowledge. One describes what has already been described a thousand times over in a light and lovely manner. The beauty of "a thousand times already told" is what I deem "kitsch." And this form of description is one which the true artist should deeply abhor. And, of course, "kitsch-beauty" is the sort of beauty which has begun to invade our modern world.[12]

Kitsch-Beauty and Knowledge-Beauty

As we have seen repeatedly, the kitsch-beauty of which Kundera speaks appeals by its beautiful illusions, by the state of ecstasy it maintains to make us forget the imperfection of human existence. The knowledge-beauty which the novel offers makes us prey, on the other hand, to the anxieties of time. "All aspects of existence which the novel discovers are discovered as beauty," Kundera writes and we know to what extent his own discoveries depend on time. What effective defence can the novel put up against kitsch and its illusions of beauty and knowledge? Laughter! "Laughter as a desperate substitute for all knowledge turned suspect."*[13]

Knowledge turned suspect—yes, in its continual effort to prune all conflictual reality of its impurities and conflicts, kitsch betrays all knowledge-beauty. Moreover, certain of Kundera's characters, such as Jakub, Sabina or Agnes, discover it only as a "betrayed beauty," as a "lost existential possibility" of which there remain but a few scattered traces. Here we are far removed from Dostoyevsky's famous visionary statement: "Beauty will save the world!"

The Circle of Happiness

Kitsch, "a stopover between being and oblivion," suspended between memory which is part of forgetting and the total negation of time, in fact signals the end of all temporal paradox. Only nostalgia for the idyll still remains, which shows that any seductiveness of kitsch-beauty experienced, more or less consciously, by Kundera's characters, is less a matter of the need for beauty than of aspirations to happiness. The desire for happiness, as Teresa understands it at the death of her dog, Karenin, is always a desire for repetition, the fiction of an eternal return. Who has never dreamt of staying the course of time? Who has never been moved, if only for a moment, by the appeal of the famous "O time, arrest your flight, and you, propitious hours, stay your course?"

As a desire for happiness, kitsch lives as a parasite on the myth, of which it duplicates not only the themes (particularly those of love and death), but also the circular structure of time which are represented, in Kundera's work, in a great variety of forms. But, above all, kitsch has been able to make the archetypal image into a privileged expression of an "idyll for all." The most extreme representation of this collective idyll remains without a doubt the island of total forgetting, an island peopled with angel-children whose bodies and souls remain bereft of all memory: utopia resonating to the stereotyped harmonies of the "music without memory" of their guitars, an Eden of nursery rhymes chanted in unison with enchanting laughter on people's lips and innocent cruelty in their hearts.

Circle, round or island are all many archetypal figures that mark the total negation of human time whose sole perspective leads to the permanence of immaturity, to thought without memory. The island where Tamina, with the memory of her adult body, can find only death seems to extend, in *The Unbearable Lightness of Being*, over the whole earth which has become the "planet of inexperience." All the variations on the old utopian dream of a world "without conflict" show clearly that kitsch demands of everyone a rhythmical harmony (the same as the one demanded of Jaromil by poetry!), the formation of a lyrical round whose dances and songs rise above life to cover with its mask of joy the shouts of disagreement of all those who do not (or who no longer) want to belong to the magic round: Tamina, Ludvik, Sabina, Mirek, the forty-year-old, Tomas, Agnes, and the narrator—Kundera are so many deniers of the idyll who see themselves excluded from the round of the "eternal throngs who travel through history." What about those who reject the idyll? They fill the prisons, their heads are cut off so that the idyll may pursue its joyous round: "The wall behind which people were imprisoned was made of verse. There was dancing in front of it. No, not a danse macabre! A dance of innocence. Innocence with a bloody smile," we read in *Life Is Elsewhere* (p. 270). The gulag, according to the narrator of *The Unbearable Lightness of Being*, can be regarded "as a septic tank used by totalitarian kitsch to dispose of its refuse" (p. 252).

Yes, only the innocence of kitsch unites like a ring, "like children, by a dance" the image of which has bewitched people for thousands of years. Madame Rafael in *The Book of Laughter and Forgetting*, for example, spends her entire life searching for a circle of men and women with whom to dance: she seeks it in Marxism, Buddhism, Taoism, psychoanalysis, in circles against abortion then for abortion, in the work of Lenin then in Zen, and so on. Kundera's irony demonstrates superbly the happiness which Madame Rafael at last finds with Gabrielle and Michèle, her students whose names are as predestined as hers: together, they ascend towards celestial heights, three archangels united by dance to the point of forming a single body, a single soul. The only thing missing for their circle to be perfect is the divine love of a Bettina von Arnim.

The rhythmic order of a circle admits of no difference, no individualism. Ludvik in *The Joke* has already learned to his cost that those who wish to live in the totalitarian idyll must give up even the tango or the boogie-woogie to "dance the round in chorus, hands resting on their neighbours' shoulders" in order to convey resoundingly their categorical agreement with its epoch's being. One false step is enough to be excluded forever from the round: a few words of disagreement as well as a simple joke. For the idyll imposes not only a "dictatorship of the heart," but also that of the agelasts! The idyll: a space beyond jokes, beyond memory and desire.

In June 1950, the narrator of *The Book of Laughter and Forgetting* reminds us, Milada Horakova, a member of the Socialist party, was hung at the same time as Zavis Kalandra, the Czech surrealist and friend of André Breton and Paul Éluard. "The dancing young Czechs, knowing that the day before, in the same city, a woman and a surrealist had been swinging from the end of ropes, were dancing all the more frenetically, because their dance was a demonstration of their innocence, in shining contrast to the guilty darkness of the two who were hanged, those betrayers of the people and its hopes" (BLF, p. 92-93). Traitors to the categorical agreement with the idyll for all, traitors to the kitsch esthetic, its ideal. Kalandra's surrealism can then be only like spitting in the face of the solidarity of all those who march, dance and laugh in perfect order under the banner of "socialist realism!"

Breton protested in vain against Kalandra's sentence. On the other hand, Éluard, the "beloved child of Prague," refused to defend the "traitor to the people" in order not to interrupt the "gigantic round" that he was then dancing with "all the socialist countries and all the communist parties." How, as we read these pages, can we not recall Jaromil's poems, so closely do they resemble the lyrical flights of oratory of Éluard's "beautiful verses on brotherhood and joy":

We shall fill innocence
With the strength that so long
We lacked
We shall no longer be alone.*

Meanwhile, to the rhythm of such idyllic "innocence," Kalandra dies, guilty of surrealism!

History as a Dimensionless Dot!

The individual in the face of history, one of the main objects of the questioning in Kundera's variations, allows him to telescope the public and private, erotic and political, maternal and totalitarian domains, and follow the slow disappearance of the border between the two a priori opposing spheres. He thereby emphasizes the proximity, the interchangeability even, of his characters' psychic mechanisms with historical mechanisms, so that one may speak, as Philip Roth suggests in relation to *Life Is Elsewhere*, of a veritable "political psychoanalysis." But Kundera also demonstrates how history itself loses its outlines and becomes a mere "dimensionless dot," a space situated beyond history.

The most effective image of such a reduction is given in *The Unbearable Lightness of Being*. Franz, the Geneva intellectual, is not, according to the narrator, a kitsch—man. This does not prevent him from letting himself be trapped by emotion to the nth power when faced with the sight of all the parades of history: one day for the Russians, another against them, one day for the Jews, another against them, and so on, in a seemingly endless repetition, as long as progress and the march continue. When on the occasion of the "Grand March" organized by the European left in which Franz takes part, when it is requested that the Western doctors be admitted onto Cambodian soil, the only reply from the other side of the border is a "stunning silence" (ULB, p. 266). Franz then suddenly understands that the borders of silence are closing in on Europe, that history with its parades, which used to represent "real" life for him, is also reaching the age of "terminal paradoxes," as Kundera names the period of the end of the modern era: the rhythm of the march is becoming faster and faster, "until finally the Grand March is a procession of rushing, galloping people and the platform is shrinking and shrinking until one day it will be reduced to a mere dimensionless dot" (ULB, p. 267).

In this most important scene where a humanitarian act is transformed into a spectacle and where the most horrible grotesque combines blood and cretinous smiles, lyricism and cruelty, Franz perceives history as a parade of misunderstandings which are leading the whole of Europe beyond its border, to the banks of total silence. He foresees, in the "dimensionless dot," the possibility of the very end of the history of Europe and, through this, the denial of all polysemies, differences and variations. Similar in this respect to Ludvik or Mirek, Franz then foresees a beyond history where all the parades are no longer anything but shadows on a "stage."

Parade: the word also represents one of the numerous semantic misunderstandings between Franz and Sabina, his Czech lover, a perfect example of the double exposure to which Kundera subjects each element in the composition of his novels. While Franz remains faithful until his death to the appeal of the rhythmic and brotherly harmonies of all the parades, for Sabina, the same image remains forever linked to communist kitsch. Behind the smiles of solidarity, behind the fists raised in unison (similar to those who condemn Ludvik in *The Joke*), she hears the order to get in step, the imperative to be identical to the image of a docile, resigned herd with no will of its own. The image of the compulsory May Day parades in her communist homeland never ceases to haunt her throughout her life. She flees, from one betrayal to the next, from all the parades which, for her, represent the very model of communist kitsch. "My enemy is kitsch, not communism" (ULB, p. 254), she replies, enraged, to all those who disguise her life of exile in hagiographic images of martyrs in an attempt, yet again, to make her fit the image of all the Czech emigrés with whom she feels no affinity whatsoever. She has known for a long time what Franz discovers only at the end of his life: that any image transformed into a kitsch model (parade or circle) reduces life to a sham and paradoxical reality to a single uniform dot.

In the Kingdom of Imagology

What happens when we have crossed the border of laughter and history? The point where history stops, says the narrator of *Immortality*, is where the reign of ideologies ends and that of imagology, which is the definitive marker of the subject's schizoid dissociation, begins. Serving up one's image to the largest audience becomes a generalized imperative as even love and death, man's last private refuges, are hounded by the eye of the cameras. Here, man is no longer "anything but his image in the eyes of others" (IMM, p. 127), dissociated conclusively from his true self. It is no coincidence that the first part of the novel is entitled "The Face": all these different faces which express, we think, the true self of all and sundry, are nothing more than another "mask of beauty" or, in the words of Immortality, a mere image of the self. The ocular metaphor which runs through his previous novels here reaches its height: the eye of God which Agnes imagines (and which Edward imagined before her in *Laughable Loves*) gives way definitively to the ubiquitous eye of the cameras. The gaze becomes institutionalized, offering everyone a mirror-image wrested from time, a sort of "instant memory" necessarily free from all desire or, if I may, a promotional identity. This is another act of manipulation by which kitsch wrests man from the movement of time (from his mortality) to condemn him to immortality, his ultimate "laughable illusion."

Among the many characters whose existence the novel explores, there is undoubtedly only Agnes, her father and Rubens who understand that there is no worse horror than "turning a second into eternity tearing someone out of the flow of time" (IMM, p. 294). Moreover, at the moment when Rubens, the latest of Kundera's Don Juans, attempts to take stock of his erotic life, he suddenly understands that memory itself takes part in the stopping of time, that memory does not film but photographs, since of his rich erotic experience he recalls only some seven fixed images, with no continuous movement: of his donjuanesque quest for knowledge to which he has devoted his entire life, there remain indeed only a few cliché-pictures of no great significance, a few souvenir-pictures, forms of forgetting and not its negation. Rubens then envies Casanova's fantastic memory, the "utopia of memory" (IMM, p. 313).

"Forgetting Being"

The text of *Immortality*, the supreme synthesis of all the semantics which unify the body of Kundera's work, is marked more than ever by forgetting. Everything in the novel submits to the totalitarian ascendency of the image, an ascendency which its maximally diffracted structure in fact attempts to subvert. The word "totalitarian" must be understood in this context, and not in the strictly ideological sense which links it to symbols of an "idyll for all" but, paradoxically, in an individual sense. The subtle semantic dislocation forcefully emphasizes that imagological kitsch (that new form of the strange human need to live more for ideas, images and abstractions than for "reality"), far from bringing man closer to his free will as one might expect in a world beyond collectivist ideologies, distances him further from them than ever. Indeed, in this age of narcissism and seductiveness, as Lipovetsky would say, where man thinks he is at last making his dream of individualism come true, the dream in fact appears as a new illusion: "What does it have to do with individualism when a camera takes your picture in a moment of agony? On the contrary, it means that an individual no longer belongs to himself" (IMM, p. 32), Agnes retorts to Paul, the lawyer for whom the modern world represents a paradise of human rights, thinking which puts him in line with that of his daughter Brigitte's generation.

Nothing but faces, says Agnes to herself as she leafs through a magazine. Nothing but laughing faces, says Rubens to himself as he looks at an album where President Kennedy's face always wears the same smile, reproduced in dozens of stereotyped copies. Rubens then reflects that even laughter no longer expresses individuality as it has been supplanted by the image by becoming the most democratic of the supplanted masks of beauty of mass media kitsch. Laughter as the uniform mask of all politicians, artists, journalists and so on, their "ideal image behind which they have decided to conceal themselves" (IMM, p. 324).

The insidious negation of all individualism which *Immortality* presents through its multiple themes and motifs, in fact stems from the obliteration of the border between private and public. The meditation on the disappearance of "shame" from the cultural map of Europe becomes an example par excellence of this. This novel clearly suggests, it seems to me, that individualism is also deserting eroticism and that the donjuanesque journey itself is nearing its end. In the "social" phase of his sex life, hearing his mistresses repeat the same words as those they say to one of his friends, Rubens suddenly has the impression that erotic language is losing its individual essence (the "one millionth-part dissimilarity" which Tomas in *The Unbearable Lightness of Being* seeks in all women), that it is becoming "democratized" and is changing into a sign of standardized social communication. With the impression that a crowd of people is watching him make love, he then attempts, with undisguised sceptical irony, a new definition of the nation: "a community of individuals, whose erotic life is united by the same game of Telephone" (IMM, p. 279). I cannot help thinking, as I reread these pages, of K. and his friend Frieda in Kafka's *The Castle*, at the moment when, after spending the night together in the village school, they wake up and find K.'s two assistants installed in their bed with all the children of the school crammed in around them to boot.

Although the men of Mirek's ideological generation in *The Book of Laughter and Forgetting* wanted to recapture their own "lost act" which, in turning against them, fulfilled their destiny in their place, those of the imagological generation no longer have to run after their "lost image." It has become their only reality, their second skin beneath which "reality no longer represents anything for anyone": life with its parade of disagreements is definitively elsewhere.

On Graphomania

The graphic epidemic which characterizes the imagological universe has its scriptural variation in the theme of graphomania which is explained in *The Book of Laughter and Forgetting* and developed in new forms in *Immortality*. Bibi, one of the customers in the bar where Tamina works, decides to write a book much as she would decide to have a scotch. She then meets the writer Banaka, the perfect prototype of what Kundera means by graphomania: "'All anyone can do,' said Banaka, 'is give a report on oneself. Anything else is an abuse of power'" (BLF, p. 124). In other words, make his "experience inside" universal, fit to be shared with the greatest number.

Graphomania, the desire of all and sundry to write books, in- evitably leads to total deafness and incomprehension, to a world where no one hears anyone any more, as individuals devote themselves entirely to listening to their own selves. According to this definition, Banaka, Bibi or the taxi driver who is writing his memoirs for posterity are graphomaniacs: they all believe in the uniqueness of their "abso- lutely original" lives and feelings which they do not want to write for themselves or their nearest and dearest but for an unknown audience. This desire to project one's self to faraway places in order to fill the void between oneself and the world is similar to the "act of immortal- ity" of Bettina who writes and rewrites her "love letters" to Goethe.

But why should Bettina and not Tamina be considered a grapho- maniac, since both write love letters? The difference is quite simple: while Tamina jealously (shamefully!) protects the intimate letters she once exchanged with her husband from any indiscreet gaze (like Tereza who used to protect—also in vain—her personal diary from the curios- ity of her mother), Bettina, for her part, is not in love with Goethe but with his fame, so that she does not hesitate to give away to the public the prefabricated image of their love. Moreover, she writes similar "love letters" to a dozen other artists (famous ones, naturally), which clearly shows the nature of the "true and divine love" which she fans within herself, and which has nothing in common with the altogether concrete love of a Tamina. The book which Bettina publishes entitled "Goethe's correspondence with a child" rests entirely on an oblitera- tive rewriting where everything (especially Goethe's standoffish letters!) is feigned in order to paint a beautiful and touching picture of a child "in love" with an immortal. Goethe, in his lifetime, no doubt never suspected that metaphors are dangerous.

But do not Goethe, Tolstoy or Kundera share the same desire, in their turn, to write books for an unknown audience? What distinguishes Banaka, Bibi or the taxi driver from a Goethe, says the narrator of *The Book of Laughter and Forgetting*, are not two different passions but two different results: on one hand, the autobiographical furor of those who launch at the world their own image transmuted into words; on the other, the exploration of the novel. A novel is not an author's confession, but an exploration of all the possibilities of existence, says Kundera, and this bias underlines his refusal to leave to posterity so much as a biographical image which can be manipulated at will. This refusal by the author, reiterated more and more clearly and in multiple ways in both *Immortality* and *Testaments Betrayed*, is playfully transcribed in the "posthumous" discussion between Goethe and Hemingway: not only do these great "immortals," even though they belong to different centuries, complain about the biographical rage (a rage where shame and respect for the author are constantly scorned) which completely obliterates their own works. However, they complain especially, with unfailing irony, about the fact that biographers only give the public kitschified, preferably "spicy," images of their lives.[14] With what devilish pleasure Goethe then surveys his "immortality," toothless and disguised as a genuine scarecrow, just to contradict the beautiful image which Bettina, as a "divine lover," wanted to set for eternity.

The end of the novel offers one of the most ironic variations on such biographical misappropriation. Indeed, his last chapter entitled, "The celebration," invites us to an almost carnavalesque party: the "celebration" of finishing the writing of his latest novel, which, moreover, the author regretfully calls *Immortality*, will not take place. Like a Trojan horse, the novel contains its own betrayals, for the border between reality and dreams, between life and the novel, is not crossed with impunity. Consequently, the author, who has become a character in his own novel, finds himself compelled, because of his imaginary self (Paul, in this case) to celebrate in fact the end of a whole era: the end of the era of works of art (and therefore of his own) and, as an indirect result, the beginning of the era of shamelessness, where only biographical gossip of famous people still attracts attention.

A World without Faces

The ocular metaphor which runs through all Kundera's work is trans-
formed here into an existential category: the "image" of the one-man
band alone in the face of his destiny. Seeing him in all his forms (gaze,
eye, camera, photo, image, and so on) is substituted for all desire,
without anyone noticing the danger which such an abduction of reality
represents.

When Agnes and her sister Laura surprise their father, at his
wife's death, tearing up all the photos of their life, Laura sees in this
an act of negation of her mother's memory.[15] Only Agnes understands
that it is an act of rejection of the "laughable illusion" which immor-
tality represents, a rejection of the posthumous "future" filled with the
clamour of memories and counterfeit photographs and biographies.
She knows that her father wants to leave behind only a peaceful
silence, the very silence he hears in the poem by Goethe on death
which he loves so much.

To grant her dying father's last wish, Agnes closes her eyes to let
him go, "slowly, unseen, for a world without faces" (IMM, p. 249), and
thereby keep the last scene of his life private, so that no prying eyes
can violate his final moment of privacy. I am thinking of Tamina's
death, so different from that of Agnes' father. However far Tamina tries
to swim from the edenic island of the angel-children to die alone,
unseen, surrounded by the silence of the sea, the children's eager gaze
recaptures her and observes her to her dying breath, *violating* her
death with their gaze, as they had once violated, into the very recesses
of her privacy, her life. The only thing missing, for Tamina's death to
resemble the one which is broadcast live on television in *Immortality*,
are the cameras.

But let us return to Agnes. At the hour of her own death pangs,
she experiences the same desire that her father had once experienced.
She hopes to die before her husband comes to join her, to go gently,
unseen. She leaves on her face, as a final sign of farewell to her
anachronistic life, only a discreet smile, as beautiful as it is incompre-
hensible.

Is it surprising that for Agnes, in total disagreement with the
imagological world around her, her "biological" father had been the
only man she had ever loved and that, in return, her "novelistic"
father feels such tenderness for her? She who, from the moment she is
born of a gesture of farewell, dreams of escaping a world overrun by
the ugliness of kitsch (visual, acoustic, olfactory) by fixing her last

gaze on the blueness of death, the silence of non-being. Moreover, Kundera ends his novel with a final nostalgic memory of the blue point which is Agnes and, in so doing, his entire novelistic score in seven movements. Never before have I read in his work passages of such troubling beauty, tinged only with the colour of disenchantment and forgetting. If the narrator-author regrets not being able to give *Immortality* the title of his previous novel *The Unbearable Lightness of Being*, it is because he knows, thanks to Agnes, that in the imagological world, "What is unbearable in life is not *being* but *being one's self.*" (*IMM*, p. 258).

On the last day of her life, travelling alone in Switzerland, Agnes experiences a moment of respite, a "pause" filled with happiness and nostalgia in which she discovers the forgotten beauty of the world of paths. She is at first surprised to find such beauty in Rimbaud: behind the image of his command "to be absolutely modern," she suddenly discovers a poet of nature and paths, quite different from the one she once read with Paul, her husband (quite different too from the one Jaromil read in *Life Is Elsewhere*): "In the blue summer evening I will go down the path, pricked by wheat, treading on the low grass . . . I will not speak, I will not think . . . And I will wander far, far like a gypsy, happy with nature as with a woman.

The Alps, that world of roads and paths, where Agnes stops after reading these lines, suddenly appear to her, as did Rimbaud's poetry, in double exposure: in two entirely different lights, two different worlds, two different beauties. It is then that she decides, before setting off again, to take one last walk, not suspecting that it will also be the last one she ever takes. Her head still filled with the echoes of Rimbaud's poems, Agnes rediscovers the beauty of paths (the beauty of discoveries, fortuities and coincidences): the betrayed beauty of Rimbaud's world, but also of her father and, beyond that, of Goethe's poem for which she has never ceased to be nostalgic since childhood. It is to that lost beauty that she now returns. Stretched out in the grass next to a stream, letting the elemental being of nature pass through her, listening for the "world without faces" of which she secretly dreams, Agnes forgets her own self, thereby discovering the blessed quietude of one who accepts the unacceptable "voice of fleeting time."

Nostalgia

From this magnificent novel of the time of Europe, I retain Agnes' nostalgia: woman-path, woman-episode, woman-smile but also woman-desire, departed with no regrets for the country without faces, without a gesture of farewell from which she was nevertheless born, because, for a long time, she has been able to slam the door in the face of kitsch, in the face of the seductiveness of all its illusions, and those of love and those of time.

Agnes obsesses me as she obsesses to the end the erotic imagination of Rubens, whose secret lover she was, as she obsesses to the last page Kundera's novelistic imagination. And I suddenly understand that, for Rubens (and for Kundera), this episode-woman sheds light on the meaning of the entire novel, a mixture of fiction and passion, of novel and life. She makes me understand that their common donjuanesque journey, erotic for Rubens and novelistic for Kundera, will henceforth only be able to follow one gaze back to the past, that there will be no more "new order" and that the "pause" will continue, filled with nostalgic memories for Agnes' lost world: "In the light with eyes shut. The dial of life."

Part Two

Variation

Chapter One

A Voyage Inside the Time of Europe[1]

[E]very writer creates his forerunners*
— J.-L. Borges

E very time I reread Milan Kundera's novelistic score in seven move-
ments, the image of a voyage appears more and more insistently
in my mind: a voyage filled with the echoes of forgotten European
paths, of crossing various times and spaces of the European novel.
But, little by little, I begin to discern much more in the work which I
hear as a single text. From its formal variations and semantic repeti-
tions, from the crossroads of their meeting where words, themes, nar-
ratives, speech and reflection extend the distorting mirror of mockery
to each other, there echoes the history of all European culture (of the
novel, music, pictures, philosophy), an outcast since then from the
modern world. Out of this there arises a nostalgic evocation of the
beauty of that entire culture, a beauty dulled by kitsch, the false mask
of beauty with which our mass media, or, to use Kundera's term,
imagological, society, adorns itself.

Letting myself be won over by Kundera's invitation to take a
return journey to a forgotten Europe also affords me the possibility of
returning to my own culture. The possibility of crossing the borders of
my own exile, inner and outer, without however falling into the trap of
sentimental nostalgia. The novelist's ironic eye prevents me implaca-
bly from doing so. I do not in any way claim this to be an all-encom-
passing definition of the semantic density of his work. I intend merely
to explore a few of the many paths which cross it, the choice of which
is a personal matter.

Notes to Chapter One of Part Two are on pp. 130-32.

As though enthralled by the inevitability of the repetition which marks the esthetic of Kundera's variation in its formal and semantic aspects, my reading can do no more than continually take up the same, to my mind, crucial themes, which emerge from it: repetition, time, love, kitsch and laughter will be given great importance and examined in their many facets. I let myself be guided by the repetition of these few themes which lead me to explore the space of their own ambiguity: the space of a border where sense and nonsense, rational and irrational, thinking and dreaming, epic intention and lyrical temptation rub shoulders. And I linger in the ambiguous space of their border each time that the laughter of the European novel, revealed by Kundera's repetition, simultaneously reveals its share of memory and forgetting, of irony and nostalgia.

Fiction and Reflection

It is commonplace to say that Kundera's novels are full of clues to his own narrative poetics: the framework of his novels is ample evidence of the development of what he himself terms the specifically novelistic essay. In addition to this, there are numerous actual critical essays in which Kundera explains the correlations between his narrative poetics and those of the entire tradition of the European novel. The latter encompasses the cultural space which extends from ancient Greece to the modern American continent and which, from Cervantes or Rabelais to Diderot, and from Kafka to Gombrowicz, Hrabal or Fuentes, preserves the playful and ironic essence of the novel as it was conceived at the dawn of the modern era. Quite obviously, the crossing of a new border is imperative here: it is important to read Kundera's novels in continuous counterpoint with one's own critical reflection. Of course, that route makes the critic's work both easier and more complicated. It makes it easier because the paths of reflection seem to be already mapped out and makes it more complicated, sometimes to the point of causing exasperation, inasmuch as the pleasure of a stroke of esthetic inspiration, as we go wherever the reading of his novels take us, has just been diminished by the discovery that, since then, the novelist has also thought of it (and has even written it!). Any pretension to uniqueness and originality becomes laughable in such cases and this is just as well as it is precisely about such pretensions that Kundera's art of combination is endlessly ironic!

I therefore necessarily examine his works of fiction also from his own critical premises, as in the double exposure so dear to the esthetic of his novels, and which lets the inverted value of each theme or idea show through. However, illustrating such a purely methodological choice should in no way suggest that his fiction originates in his critical thought. Quite the contrary, it is the very technique of his variation, which, through its interrogative construction, "turns its gaze towards Europe's past." Like a semantic anaphora, variation cuts obliquely through the significant thematic spaces of the European novel (but also of music, painting and philosophy) and in so doing demands an intertextual reading. It is only through such a dialogical reading that all the examined themes are able to reveal their essential polysemy and ambiguity. This allows me to indulge in the pleasure demanded by Barthes: the pleasure of interpreting a text not so much to give it meaning but to appreciate the plurality of which it is composed.[2]

The Art of the Novel

The very first essays which Kundera devoted to the European novel, collected under the title *The Art of the Novel*, emphasized in many respects the link between his critical reflection and his specifically novelistic meditation insofar as the link is a part of the form itself of the collection. Indeed, the seven movements of the collection summon the echo of his arithmetical (unconscious? donjuanesque?) passion which gives a significant stamp to his novel cycle. The seven essays, formerly published elsewhere in response to a variety of situations (articles, interviews, personal dictionary, the 1985 Jerusalem Prize address), could, after all, have formed a heterogeneous whole. Paradoxically, the collection reveals all the more the underlying coherence of Kundera's esthetic reflection and sensibility. By referring us in an almost subliminal way to the composition of the texts of his novels, the seven movements of the essay remind us that Kundera strives always for a heterogeneous, achronological and acausal synthesis of narrative and emotional spaces.

Indeed, the mirror of *The Art of the Novel* confers on the genre not its history, past or what is to come, but rather its own wasted possibilities, and even the exhaustion of what constitutes its essence and specificity. In part seven of the essay, the spirit of the novel confronts the spirit of the times in their radically different aspects: on one hand, an unceasing quest for ambiguity, relativity, irony and its epic laughter and, on the other, the sentimentalist complacency of the lyrical age-lasts toiling earnestly to build a kingdom of kitsch as seductive as it is compensatory. Is this not the same image which, in spite of the difference in genre, emerges from all his novels, especially *Immortality*?

Whether it is a matter of the critical eye of the essayist or the ironic eye of the novelist, the many different processes which weave his work together always underline the polyphony of existence and are thereby programmatically opposed to the reductionism of kitsch.

Moreover, behind the surface arithmetical sign there is revealed the deep structure of the essay which reproduces the variational process proper to Kunderian fiction by telescoping the various possibilities of the novel as a genre from diverging points of view and with the aid of a variety of discourses.[3] The even—numbered chapters are devoted to Kundera's art itself, while the Central European novel occupies the odd-numbered chapters (3-Broch and 5-Kafka), which are the intervals left by the former. The whole is placed as if in brackets within chapters one and seven ("The Legacy of Cervantes" and "The Novel and Europe"). The dialogical resonance of Kundera's art of the novel with a certain esthetic tradition of the Central European and European novel is thus a part of the very core of the book. Although *The Art of the Novel* originates in a personal vision of the novelist, the fact remains that, by integrating three chapters which focus on his work into the composition of the collection, he poses, ironically, as a reader of his own art of the novel. This is the reversed image of the double narrative authority which the author later acquires, as both narrator and one of the characters, in his latest novel *Immortality*.

The Art of Combination

Those who, with *The Art of the Novel*, expected a chronological history or even a theory of the novel could not but be disappointed: in relinquishing all linear perspective, the very structure of the collection dismantles, in a way that could hardly be more novelistic, any impulse towards "progress." It is as though Kundera were suggesting that it is futile to construct a linear history of the European novel and that only a variational approach can define its experience and give an account of the journey of its esthetic values and essential playfulness. Attempting to make his critical reflection historical and chronological would therefore be as ridiculous and nonsensical as wanting to reconstruct a linear plot from his novelistic variations.

Without wishing to make a forced, mechanical correlation between fiction and reflection in Kundera's work, I cannot help letting myself be caught up in the interplay of coincidences and imagining that there exists a secret link between the seven parts of his essay and his seven novels. It is not mere chance that the semantics of the interplay between illusion and reality in *Laughable Loves* corresponds to the thought on the playfulness of Cervantes. Or that the *Book of Laughter and Forgetting* (his fifth) evokes the same memoriless world as Kafka's, as does chapter five of *The Art of the Novel*; that the "Seventy-one words" of chapter six of the essay find a formal and semantic echo in the "words misunderstood" of *The Unbearable Lightness of Being*; that *Immortality*, the seventh and latest of his novels, as well as part seven of *The Art of the Novel* evoke, each in its own way, the struggle between kitsch and the novel of which Broch spoke.

Testaments Betrayed, Kundera's latest essay, composed not in seven but in nine parts, constitutes even clearer evidence of the closeness between his critical reflection and the semantics of his novelistic variations, the precedence even, of the latter over the former. Even the title suggests that all reflection in the essay consists of another "voyage inside the time of Europe," in a form of irony other than that to be found in his novels, especially in *Immortality*. Indeed, as if to intensify Rubens', his latest Don Juan's, reflection, but also that of the narrator of part seven of the novel, the gaze of the essayist of *Testaments Betrayed* is stamped with an equally ironic nostalgia in the face of a past betrayed by memory and deserted by laughter, in the face of its "beauty betrayed" by time. For beyond the compositional links between the art of music and the art of the novel explored in the essay, beyond the esthetic testaments of artists such as Stravinski, Kafka, Janacek, Gombrowicz, Beckett, Hemingway, Fuentes, Sollers or Rushdie, Kundera reveals a much larger betrayal. Behind the testaments betrayed by friends, translators, interpreters or critics, Kundera gives us a glimpse of the betrayal, of all the basic principles, of the specificity even, of our "novel society" as Cioran terms the European culture of the modern era, a unique heritage to which Kundera wishes to remain faithful. Kundera states in the most explicit way possible this time that the novel represents for him more than a mere literary genre among others. Being a novelist implies for Kundera an existential attitude founded on constant questioning of the individual's freedom and identity, on an attitude capable of "suspending all moral judgement" to the benefit of relativity and doubt, the space par excellence of knowledge which is still possible and, because of this, resistant to all categorical agreement with any politics, religion, ideology or morality whatsoever: "Are you a Communist, Mr. Kundera?" "No, I'm a novelist." "Are you on the left or the right?" "Neither, I'm a novelist" (TB, p. 158).

Shame: An Existential Metaphor of the Modern Era

The forgotten paths rediscovered in the novel's esthetic of times past, the freedom of composition, the coexistence of different eras, humour, humanity's identity, sentimentalism, betrayal, graphomania or biographical furor, are all themes and motifs which reoccur, in *Testaments Betrayed*, like critical resonances of his specifically novelistic essays and variations.[4] But above all I recognize in them a theme which suddenly makes the semantic closeness even more obvious between a Kundera-essayist and a Kundera-novelist who left his mark particularly on *Immortality* and who, with the new essay, underlines even further the necessity of reading his collected works—on a semantic level, I mean—as a single text. I have in mind the theme of shame: Shame is one of the key notions of the Modern Era, the individualistic period that is imperceptibly receding from us these days; shame: an epidermal instinct to defend one's personal life; to require a curtain over the window; . . . We enter adulthood through the rebellion of shame (TB, pp. 259-60). Shame (and its disappearance in the twentieth century) appears as a crucial existential metaphor of the age of modernity both in *Immortality* and *Testaments Betrayed*.

Far from being associated with some kind of individual prudishness, the exploration of the *border* between shame and shamelessness and, especially, its insidious disappearance in our time, signals in Kundera's work the end itself of individual freedom, the end of respect for one's private life, leading indirectly to the institutionalized rape of writers' esthetic will, as well as the establishing of compulsory voyeurism which gives legitimacy to the worst anthropological scandal of this supposedly democratic century. The disappearance of shame from the face of Europe and, as a consequence, the discontinuation of the donjuanesque journey which, let us not forget, remains the metaphor of the journey itself of Kundera's variation, is what Rubens had already observed in *Immortality*[5] and what the narrator of *Testaments Betrayed* re-examines in concreto, through the lives and works of several of this century's great authors. In the concluding parts of the novel and essay, texts which, however, are generically (and ironically!) so different, it is the same "celebration": that of the end of an era in which life and authors' works have not yet suffered the betrayals which Kundera terms kitschifying interpretations. For him, each of these betrayals harbours its share of shamelessness. But in addition, by depicting just as many obliterations of laughter, humour and therefore of the relativity vital to our "novel society," they take aim not only at art but at reality itself and thereby make insidious preparation for the day when "Panurge no longer makes people laugh."

For an Esthetic of the Palimpsest

In the esthetic metaphor of the three periods which Kundera develops in his *Improvisation in Homage to Stravinski*,[6] the question of laughter as the very spirit of the European novel remains essential. By comparing the history of European (thousand-year-old) music and that of the novel (four centuries), Kundera emphasizes the asynchronicity of their esthetic caesura (the eighteenth century for music, between the eighteenth and nineteenth for the novel) in order to demonstrate that the profound changes regulating the rhythm of the history of art are not the concern of sociology but of the intrinsic esthetic of each of the arts. The caesura which, for Kundera, signals the second period of the novel, in fact traces that border beyond which the spirit of laughter and non-seriousness (that of Cervantes, Rabelais, Sterne or Diderot) is suppressed by the esthetic of seriousness and its imperative of verisimilitude. In their crossings of the border of time, the great novelists of the twentieth century in general, and Kundera's variational repetitions in particular, hasten to follow above all in the footsteps of the laughter of the novel's first period, listening attentively to the European novel's appeal of the past. Listening not to the succession of works of which it is made up, but to the polyphony which Kundera discerns in the playfulness in as early an author as Cervantes and which constitutes for him the basis of all the possibilities explored in his own art of combination. Kundera definitely belongs in this respect to the tradition of this century's great novelists whom he terms post-Proustian: the tradition of the third period which, from Kafka, Musil, Broch and Gombrowicz to Fuentes, Puig or Hrabal, strives to rediscover the esthetic of the first period, to make a playful retranscription of memory, losing itself in a palimpsest which has become illegible. A journey into the "well of the past": this is the metaphor of *Testaments Betrayed* which best captures the very essence of the esthetic ambition in the third period in the history of the European novel.

As one might suspect, there is no question whatsoever with these novelists, of naively recirculating certain artistic forms or of personally rejecting the entire nineteenth-century esthetic. The meaning of such an appeal of the past is much more important and Kundera explains this clearly:"The point of the rehabilitation is more general: to *redefine* and *broaden* the very notion of the novel: to resist the *reduction* worked by the nineteenth-century's aesthetic of the novel;

to give the novel its *entire* historical experience for a grounding" (TB, p. 75).

Having as a basis the novel's entire historical experience demands that each novelist make a certain number of choices among the very many potential paths to be taken. Kundera's choices are to be found in the four appeals which come down to him from history and to which he says he is particularly sensitive: the appeal of play, the appeal of dream, the appeal of thought and the appeal of time (AN, pp. 15-16). The entire innovative esthetic value of his art of the novel is part of the formal and semantic combinatorial analysis of these various appeals to the past but, above all, of the phenomenological light they shed on this century of terminal paradoxes.

The Appeal of Time

"The period of terminal paradoxes incites the novelist to broaden the time issue beyond the Proustian problem of personal memory to the enigma of collective time, the time of Europe, Europe looking back on its own past, weighing up its history like an old man seeing his whole life in a single moment" (AN, p. 16). Like a bridge constructed over different periods, close in this respect to Carlos Fuentes of *Terra Nostra*, this is the voyage of the playful transcription which Kundera's variation makes of the elements chosen in the course of his journey to the past. But the beauty of knowing the novel revealed in each of the variations arises from the colliding impact past and present: ". . . The thought then came to him that beauty is a spark that flashes when, suddenly, across the distance of years, two ages meet. That beauty is an abolition of chronology and a rebellion against time" (BLF, p. 73).

Moreover appeals of play, of dream and of thought take on their true meaning in the interplay with time, at the level of the narrative and discursive structure of his novels. It is also the appeal of time which shows unmistakably that the esthetic value of Kundera's *chez-soi* is to be found not only in Czech or Central European literature, but also in the history of the four centuries of the European novel as Kundera has been able to encompass them in his seven novelistic movements. After all, the esthetic value of a work does not have a great deal to do with its creator's national or regional attachment.

It would be equally futile to seek in his novels some kind of disguised autobiography in the canonical sense of the term, since all the temporal elements and techniques used, as well as his set of themes, in fact work towards destroying any chronology and thus any spirit of graphomania. The conclusion of *Immortality* draws attention more insistently than ever to the bias in favour of an ironic reading insofar as Kundera portrays himself simultaneously in the work as author, narrator and character, thereby rendering ambiguous the very border between real, narrative and discursive time.[7] In company with his own imaginary egos, Kundera-author witnesses, with unconcealed ironic nostalgia, the death of the European novel (and of his own), the celebration of a new age in which only novelists' biographies (also rewritten!) still succeed in passing the test of immortality. But this new immortality no longer amounts to anything but their new posthumous death, to a supreme act of forgetting which heralds the end of an era in which the artist lived simultaneously in all periods.

The Appeal of Play

The appeal of play inherited by Kundera from the history of the European novel gives rise to the resounding echo of quixotic adventures which was already in search of the border between illusion and reality tirelessly explored by Kundera in his work. On the same border he drives out the laughter arising from each encounter between his playful narration and the seriousness of the battle which increasing numbers of modern Don Quixotes fight against the windmills of illusion. In so doing, he also turns his attention towards two great playful novels of the eighteenth century: Sterne's *Tristram Shandy* and Diderot's *Jacques le Fataliste*. In their endless episodic and therefore achronological narrative digressions, obeying the sole imperative of pleasure of the narrative interplay, Kundera sees the discovery of the European novel's formal humour. It is here that the playful part of his own variational esthetic draws its initial inspiration. Moreover, his theatrical variation on Diderot's novel constitutes a double marker of the formal relationship.

But Kundera does not only explore the formal aspect which links him, across two centuries, to Diderot. He makes laughter itself the central semantic object of his own novelistic repetition, his playful digressions and meditations. His very first titles heralded such "trial by laughter."[8] Laughter becomes indissociable from the (formal and semantic) repetition which fuels all his work. I am therefore able to follow the traces of the theme of laughter with its many metamorphoses through the scores of his novels, while at the same time hearing the echo of the very history of laughter of all European culture. But in them I also perceive laughter to be a result of structure, the very principle of the novel conceived as an ironic and playful genre par excellence.

There is therefore no question here of some abstract or universal idea of laughter, irony or comedy, but of their existential exploration in the specific context of the European novel, of the art which is "born of God's laughter." The laughter which Kundera also examines in our own age is given great importance in his critical reflection, and simultaneously, in his novelistic variation. This allows him to define the paradox itself of the comic in our Kafkan world, for he does not *"accompany* the tragic, not at all, but kills it in the egg." Indeed, if tragedy brings consolation for Kundera, comedy is more cruel, for it suddenly sheds light on our existence in all its insignificance. Consequently, the genius of laughter lies for him in the discovery of "an unknown realm of the comic," especially that of history and sexuality (AN, p. 126). History and sexuality, both often telescoped together in the narrative framework of his fictional texts, become targets of choice for Kundera's corrosive laughter.

Variation and Laughter

For Kundera, the novel is above all "the great prose form in which an author thoroughly explores, by means of experimental selves (character), some great themes of existence" (AN, p. 142). Again, it is laughter which, among all his themes, expresses most sharply the very essence of human existence in its relativity, polysemy and ambiguity. Seizing that laughter in its complex thematic and structural dimension, therefore becomes indissociable from the melodic developments (textual and intertextual) traced by his variational journey. Moreover, Kundera underlines the dual importance of the semantics of laughter by linking the theme closely to the mechanism itself of repetition, which is both a basic principle of his own esthetic form and a questioning of existence. I see the most innovative value of his novel's esthetic as being in this variational synthesis, hence my constant return to the borders where the dynamic synthesis ravels and unravels each time they are crossed.

In *The Book of Laughter and Forgetting*, the variational interplay with the theme of laughter even marks its compositional function: it becomes the only link among the novel's seven heterogeneous movements which, without it, would be deprived of its phenomenological vision of the world and thus its extraordinary ironic dimension. Variation represents here, rather as in Schonberg's music, the most extreme form of repetition. Moreover, *Laughable Loves* can be read in a similar way and for this reason, it is included in my reading as one of the seven opuses of his work.

Because of his particular process of repetition, Kundera is similar to a good many European authors who, in different forms, have recourse to the same paradoxical logic. But his novels also carry, on more than one account, the echo of an entire European philosophical tradition, since the problematic of repetition is represented as one of the fundamental existential questions and one of the basic elements of all European culture.[9] In this regard, the repetition in multiple forms of the theme of laughter in Kundera's work seems exemplary, for it results in two opposite, even extreme, outcomes: on one hand, imitation, resemblance, identity and on the other, difference, dissimilarity and plurality. On one hand, the absolute answers and certainties of forgetting (totalitarianism, kitsch, idyll); on the other, the diffracted universe of uncertainties, doubts, questionings of memory (relativity, novel, variation). On one hand, the "Platonic repetition" which produces the perfect and imitative harmony of the angels' laughter, and, on the other, "Nietzschian repetition"[10] allowing the discord of the Devil's laughter to burst out. With the first repetition, we are still in a tragedy; with the second, we are already crossing the border into farce. In fact, the variational work with the theme of laughter brings off in Kundera's work a perfect synthesis of all the virtualities inscribed between the two extreme poles of repetition. Such exploration of the possibilities clearly shows that the Kunderian esthetic, far from being governed by the dual principle of language and the world, stems openly from their multiform and polysemic construction. Here we also find the phenomenological essence of his art of the novel in which variation becomes the instrument par excellence of an ironic knowledge of existence.

Restating and Rewriting

Jacques and His Master, Kundera's theatrical variation on Diderot's novel *Jacques le Fataliste*, represents without a doubt the most extreme case of exploring the possibilities of the European novel. Two hundred years after Diderot, the laughter of Jacques and his master rings out once more, more fatalistic, more sceptical but, also more necessary than ever. That laughter, amplified by *Jacques and his Master*, is in fact the product of a variation which introduces us to the complex problematic of formal repetition, that of *rewriting* whose synthetic esthetic ("everything has been written simultaneously") allows the meeting of two ages, two writers and two genres. The appeal of play and the appeal of time converge. Between Diderot's text and its Kunderian repetition, an essentially Donjuanesque journey of repetition is mapped out, where writing also means rewriting and where the paradox implied by the very act of such rewriting (both writing and reading, forgetting and memory) amplifies the echo of its own laughter.

One has only to turn the opening pages of *Jacques le Fataliste* to see that it is an infinite narrative and discursive adventure, with no beginning or end, with no other borders than those of its own ambiguity where all values can reverse their role, where Jacques and his master indulge in joyful verbal sparring with the aid of more or less disguised quotations (Jacques quotes the captain who had quoted Spinoza and so on), and questions left unanswered which interrupt the telling of their story in order to begin it again, to restate it.

All the playfulness of Kunderian variation is very much part of what follows in the adventure. Moreover, even the interventions of the narrator and his libertine manner of addressing the reader or his characters finds an obvious echo here. Diderot-narrator is also a reader of Sterne, just as Kundera is a reader of Diderot, Sterne, Cervantes. Thus on both sides a surprising textual labyrinth is created where playful speech and critical speech become inseparable: their interlacing produces a playful logic in which all the elements of composition, as heterogeneous as they may be, as episodic as they may appear, are linked intertextually by the exploration of the central theme, that of the loves of Jacques, the master and Madame de la Pommeray. Obviously, grasping such a narrative labyrinth which Kundera's art pushes to the limits in *Immortality*, requires the most attentive of readings. The novelist's sly pleasure? Undoubtedly, but above all a desire to counter any possibility of reduction in the knowledge of the novel to a mere adaptation, or even to a televisual or cinematographic ersatz filled with non-essential elements. The categorical refusal of any reduction of a work of art to a mere adaptation becomes even more explicit in Kundera's subsequent texts: "If a person is still crazy enough to write novels nowadays and wants to protect them, he has to write them in such a way that they cannot be adapted, in other words, in such a way that they cannot be retold" (IMM, pp. 237-38). Jacques and his master were saying the same thing even then!

Playful Transcription

Kundera's variation on Diderot's text thereby becomes, as Kundera says himself, a double homage to variation: variation on Diderot which, moreover, uses the technique of variation. This play differs from his novelistic texts insofar as it is a particular and direct playful transcription of another text (a variation in the singular on Diderot's novel). What is more, the fact that it is rewritten is emphasized by the author's preface, by his "Introduction to a variation." The text can be read, in Kundera's work as a whole, as a paradigm of this synthetic rewriting which is the esthetic of his novelistic variation and his crossing of borders, including the one between different genres.

On the other hand, in the dialogical space of his novels, the semantic echoes of the European novel which can be heard (of Kafka, Broch, Musil, Gombrowicz, etc.) are integrated into the structure of the whole to the point of being practically dissolved and barely discernible from the Kunderian melody. The metamorphic work of his variation with the dominant themes of European culture and literature allows us to read his novels, but especially *Immortality*, as the novel of Europe, or even as a playful transcription of the very essence of its culture.

As a variation in the singular, *Jacques and his Master* states in a major key what his novels suggest in the minor: the imperative to restate, vary and combine in a creative way what has already been written in the European novel, in order to retain the memory. The bias towards an essentially mnesic art of combination, which Kundera shares with a good many contemporary novelists (especially Hrabal and Fuentes) is in marked contrast to that other repetition which, for its part, offers only the affirmation of a single meaning and a single truth, so that order, and beyond that, forgetting and death, may reign: forgetting the relativity which characterizes the European novel, the death of its laughter and of all existential ambiguity. On the palimpsest of the "great scroll" deleted by our modern culture, *Jacques and His Master* rewrites what Kundera so admires in the history of the novel's first period: its relativity and the doubt necessary for the survival of its ironic essence.

Border

The same event may prove totally commonplace for one person, but be charged with significance for another. We are in a space undermined by paradoxes which Terry Eagleton very aptly terms that of semiotic paranoia.[11] Thanks to the internal polysemic tension with which Kundera invests every sign (every word, theme or situation), the border becomes the ironic centre of his entire esthetic of the novel. Only from this border can laughter break out and, with it, the echo of its grotesque caricature. The dual laughter revealed by crossing the space separating its opposite poles points to the reversibility of the meaning and value of our existence, of all things human, be they individual or collective. The structural elements of Kundera's work seem to fall into place in order that all rhetoric born of conviction be replaced by a rhetoric born of derision. It is as though we were hearing the echo of Nietzsche's words, for whom it is not anger but laughter which kills: "Come, let us kill the spirit of heaviness!"*[12]

This practice of variation carries within it one of the harshest criticisms of modern communication: a sharp criticism of all the semantic deceptions and illusions of our language, of our thoughts and speech. But it also makes us take part, alongside its imaginary egos (and this is no doubt where Kundera disturbs his reader the most) in the unmasking of the ideological and imagological manipulation of which we are all more or less consenting actors: he manipulating of our own values and meanings which we naively thought, in the name of make-believe free will, we gave to our existence. Concrete examples of Kundera's criticism of language are legion. Let us merely recall here all the word-themes (joke, laughter, forgetting, litost, lyricism, love, gesture, kitsch, etc.) which Kundera's variation explores in the infinite possibilities of their semantic metamorphoses. His numerous "words misunderstood," far from being limited to a chapter in *The Unbearable Lightness of Being*, run right through his work like so many elliptical signs of a widespread incommunicability. Through continual excursions into the semantic crossroads of each one of his words, Kundera reinvests the language with a little of its forgotten polysemy, relativity and laughter. While Kundera affirms, like Broch and Musil, that for him knowledge constitutes the sole moral code of the novel, its only passion for him lies in the laughter and irony to which it gives rise. Like an illusionist Don Juan, eyeing himself skeptically in the mirror of his own repetitions, the laughter which bursts forth from Kundera's variation shares the same knowledge (how anti-romantic and anti-lyrical it is!) with the Devil in *Doctor Faustus*: they both know that real passion exists only in ambiguity and in the form of irony.[13]

The Appeal of Dream

Kundera's passion for ambiguity also draws its inspiration from Novalis' ambition to fuse dreams with reality, something which was first accomplished in Kafka's novels. However, Kundera's variation offers a contrapuntal rather than a fusing relationship between dreams and reality. Think, for example, of Tereza's dreams in *The Unbearable Lightness of Being*, of her obsessional dreams understood as so many poems on death which reveal the true face of kitsch, that which is, in fact, only a "screen to conceal death."[14] Or of *Life Is Elsewhere*, where the interplay between dreams and reality blurs any border between the two semantic universes: the poet Jaromil's reality is created from dreams, while the dreams of Xavier, his own imaginary alter ego, appear as so many fragments of a (revolutionary and loving) compensatory reality. On the narrow border between Jaromil's reality and Xavier's dreams, between the self and the image of the self which Jaromil would like to project onto the scene of his historic and private life, values become indiscernible.

It can be said that, in the masterpiece novels created under the sign of the art of combination, the art of the dream always reveals the pure inner truth of a being by extending to him a temporal mirror which lacks any causal logic. Kundera's realism is quite different from this, for he also knows that in the implausibility of dreams, "realism can be a deceptive disguise of true reality.[15]

The Appeal of Thought

The novel as the supreme intellectual synthesis, as the sum of knowledge where all the elements of existence, real and unreal, rational and irrational, narrative, meditative, discursive, oneiric and others, are apparently mobilized by an art of combination and counterpoint par excellence. This is the appeal which Kundera hears in Musil and Broch, especially in *The Man without Qualities* of the former and also in *The Sleepwalker* of the latter. This is also the inspirational ground of the cognitive part of his variational esthetic, a part which he himself refers to, let us remember, as a specifically novelistic essay. The two faces, the playful and the cognitive, of his variation are never separated here but are seen simultaneously, as though they were an integral part of the double exposure to which the variational process subjects all its themes, situations and characters.

The formal lightness on themes as weighty as death, love, fortuity, destiny, necessity and a number of others, in fact reveals a passion for the concrete which Kundera shares with Central European culture: the themes are always embodied in a particular existential possibility and never developed in a purely abstract fashion. One must therefore never think, as one might when thinking of such titles as *The Unbearable Lightness of Being* or *Immortality*, that we are dealing with "philosophical novels." Kundera's form of playful meditation does not affirm but questions and through this, etymologically speaking, shows itself to be essentially ironic. Moreover, as soon as it sees itself subjected to the game of the novel, all philosophical reflection changes its meaning and becomes hesitation and hypothesis. Thus freed from any vague institutional impulses, it takes part in the vertigo of fortuity and the imaginary to which variation subjects any semantic element. Indeed, Kundera is not a philosopher but a novelist and we can say of him what Musil thought of his character in *The Man without Qualities*: "He was not a philosopher. Philosophers are violent people who, for want of an army at their disposal, subjugate the world by enclosing it in a system."[16] And what if philosophy's true freedom were played out solely in the ironic space of the novel?

As an exploration of the possibilities of existence, Kundera's variation evokes not only the musical analogies which are explained at length in his work, but also an entire tradition of Central European philosophical thought, in this case Husserlian phenomenology. The latter's world vision has since inspired numerous Czech creators and thinkers, beginning with the Mukarovsky's whole school of esthetics and ending with Patocka's philosophy. Kundera's novelistic variation surely constitutes the esthetic mode closest to phenomenological thought, to that other imaginary variation as imagined by Husserl: a way of exploring the world, the essence of human life, the ontological essence even, of being. It is perhaps this aspect itself which best reveals, if I may say, Kundera's Central European unconscious. Whatever the case may be, in the name of his variational esthetic, he is surely, among the novelists of today, the one who has best been able to capture the phenomenological poetry of existence.

Variations on Central Europe

Beyond the formal implications of Kundera's response to the appeal of thought, I discern an entire semantic dimension proper to Central European novels. Through his passion for the concrete, an entire anti-lyrical and antikitsch dimension comes through, a dimension which he shares with the demystifiers of lyrical facades and illusions such as Kafka, Ladislav Klima, Hasek, Musil, Broch, Gombrowicz, and many others. A particular range of themes and motifs, lyricism, immaturity, inexperience, illusion, kitsch and sentimentalism, become in a way their common semantic denominator.

The lyrical, romantic or kitsch attitude thus becomes in Kundera's work the determining element of the existential code of his imaginary selves. The poet Jaromil in *Life Is Elsewhere* is without a doubt the most obvious example of this and it seems to me regrettable that the novelist did not retain the title he had originally envisaged: *The Lyrical Age*. I read the novel as a variation-homage to Witold Gombrowicz, to his sarcastic criticism of sentimental lyricism permeated with a typically Central European grotesqueness. Think of the outbreak of silliness in *Ferdydurke* where lyricism sets itself up as the main target of Gombrowicz's satire on immaturity, on youth and its modernist imperative. Kundera's poet Jaromil obeys the same imperative, even if his silliness becomes more politicized, from whence comes his greatest danger: witness the final fusion between the poet and the executioner which Jaromil will come to embody for the greater glory of his poetry and his narcissistic satisfaction. This novel represents, next to Flaubert's *Madame Bovary* and Gombrowicz's *Fedydurke*, represents the most devastating criticism of a certain poetry which sets up all feeling (loving, revolutionary, religious) as an absolute value.[17]

The logical outcome of the corrosive demystification of lyrical illusions which the epic and *episodic* esthetic of Kunderian variation pursues relentlessly, is the questioning of a related and also typically Central European theme: that of man's irresponsibility and the crime which is its most exaggerated face. Is Jakub in *The Farewell Party* responsible for Ruzena's murder, since he will ultimately never know whether the pill he slipped into her tube of painkillers was really poison or the mere illusion of her own freedom to put an end to her life? Is the poet Jaromil responsible for having denounced his girlfriend's brother in the name of an abstract ideal of revolution? Are communists excused by their own ignorance? This is the question Tomas raises in *The Unbearable Lightness of Being*, using as evidence the story of Oedipus who, for his part, "did not know either" and yet put out his eyes before leaving for Thebes. The examination of crime, punishment and responsibility runs so deeply through the novels of Central Europe that it can be seen as one of their central themes. It is present in the novels of Kafka (*The Trial*), Ladislav Klima *Prince Sternenhoch's Suffering*), Robert Musil (*The Man without Qualities*), Hermann Broch (*The Sleepwalkers*), Witold Gombrowicz (*Pornography*), Tibor Déry (*Mr. G. A. in X.*), Odon von Horvath (*A Child of Our Time*), Heimito von Doderer (*Every Man a Murderer*), Pavel Kohout (*The Hangwoman*), and the list could go on indefinitely. It is therefore not surprising that the theme is taken up by Kunderian variation in several of his texts and that, in *The Farewell Party* and *The Unbearable Lightness of Being* especially, it leads to a meditation on the unbearable lightness of crime in this age of terminal paradoxes.

The Individual and History

Beyond those themes, Kundera examines the question of man caught in the trap of contemporary history. We are not dealing at all here with a portrait of the times since history itself is examined in his novels as one existential situation among many. Moreover, in the Central European view of history, man appears as an object of history and not as a Sartrian subject. History itself becomes in its turn the privileged target of the interplay between the novel and its irony. Kundera's heroes know full well that they are merely performers of previously written texts and that even these texts can be rewritten and modified *a posteriori*.

The view of history in Central European novels is far from tragic. Resistant to all psychologism, destructive of all linearity worthy of a great historical account, such are the characteristics of the gaze "from below" which is brought to bear here on "the great, the divine, the rational." This particular view becomes the very basis of what can be termed the Central European grotesque. Structurally, the narrative is broken up in many ways, its perspective becomes plural, anecdotal and episodic. In short, history often reveals itself as a spectacle of grotesque games and adventures which, when all is said and done, are of no great historical importance and where comedy, it will be remembered, is not by the side of tragedy but "destroys it in the egg."

Kafka seems to turn his back on history the very day that the First World War is declared, noting in his *Journal* "afternoon at swimming pool," as Kundera reminds us, while for Hasek the adventures of his characters through the same war are no longer anything but mere historical excursions. The future will not take place, we know, either for Kraus or for Musil's characters, and, for Broch, history is quite simply devoid of any axiological value. Without, of course, forgetting Ludvik in *The Joke* for whom it is no longer anything but a large system of errors: and what if history were joking, he finally wonders.

The Small Concealed History

But if history itself is no longer anything but cause for laughter, what should be man's position in the face of it? Thumbing his nose at it or standing to attention? In underwear or in ceremonial uniform? If we agree with Vaclav Behloradsky[18] that the specificity of Central European culture is a reflection on the absurd effort of cramming all the vital anarchic energies into a uniform (in both the literal and metaphorical sense of the term), and therefore of hiding all that is nocturnal and other than the law, the novels of Central Europe, from Kafka to Kundera, can appear as a procession of men in underwear or nightshirts, with obvious disrespect and unfailing derision.

The refusal of the novel to see history strutting about in its ceremonial rags, the refusal to hide life's disorder under a uniform, is signalled by an irreverent desire to reveal a glimpse, if only for a moment, of the grotesqueness of what is hidden beneath. The grotesque scenes in which history comes on stage in its underwear are many: in *The Trial*, Joseph K. is arrested in his nightshirt and, in *The Castle*, K. discusses, in a civil servant's bed, the outcome of his existential quest; the good soldier Schweik hears the official mass for the troops who must leave for the Great War (which is not their war!) in his nightshirt and underwear while Joachim von Pasenow in Broch's *The Sleepwalkers* takes jealous care that nothing shows beneath his ceremonial coat because, for him, the uniform is like a second skin and its true function "is most certainly nothing more than to display and rule on the order of the world"; on the other hand, history—the communist revolution!—comes on stage in the life of Kundera's Jaromil in his underwear, but it is because "the hideousness of the underwear" is a compulsory uniform of his time (LIFE, p. 239).

Life demands its rights and, as soon as we let it out of our sight, is back in force to tear down the facade of all the lyrical illusions of the world of order, perfection and purity. Moreover, as soon as a little individual history decks itself out in idyllic and showy costumes, it barely escapes derision. From that point of view, it would be tempting to put together a small anthology of scatological scenes from novels which would be set down as so many ridiculous stains on human existence. I am thinking, as an example, of Marinette in Hrabal's *Too Loud a Solitude*, of the ridiculous mercenary angel of artists whose glorious destiny is constantly stained by his own pooh. But I am thinking above all of the numerous scatological variations which punctuate Kundera's work like so many fragments of a life demanding its rights, beginning with Helena's failed "scatological suicide" in *The Joke* and ending with that of Stalin's son ("died for shit's sake") in *The Unbearable Lightness of Being*. Here the scatological dimension becomes an important factor of the novel's derision and irony, its main function being to pierce the many masks of beauty and dull the rosy colours with which the time of the (private and collective) idyll disguises the times of human existence.

Of Double Repetition

The esthetic value of Kundera's work seems to fit conclusively into in his vision of existential time which especially marks his playful and protean meditation on repetition. The formal interplay of his own variations confers a repetitive questioning on every level of the text— semantic, semiotic, narrative and structural. But the problematic of repetition, to which the themes, characters and stories are no less subject, is always viewed through the double exposure of its conflicting poles: on one hand, mimetic (Platonic) repetition and, on the other, variational (Nietzschean) repetition. Yet again, the very venture of Kundera's exploration lies in the space of the *border* which both separates and connects them. It is as though we are reminded that our existence cannot escape, any more than that of the novel, the inevitability of the double exposure and its paradoxes.

The repetitions represent the motivating force itself of the poetic of Kunderian variation conceived of as a continual, but always differentiating, renewal of the same object (theme, word, motif) in order to invest it each time with a new meaning, a different temporal light. As an indirect result, the themes are enriched in the interplay of the repetition and from it, draw a meditative element and consequently, a maximum semantic density. Thus, Kundera's entire semantic foundation is explicitly connected to time, split between memory and forgetting which represent its limits.

Even the theme of laughter does not escape the double repetition, quite the contrary. Kundera makes laughter coincide with memory and forgetting, makes laughter emerge from forgetting itself thereby indicating the possibility of its own finiteness. In *Immortality*, laughter no longer exists except under a compulsory grimace, like a mere physiological convulsion.

A Potential Don Juan

What are the possibilities for man caught in the trap of this double repetition and the seductiveness it exerts on him? Kundera's genius resides in having been able to make the epic adventure of his writing coincide with the questioning of the very essence of our lives, the theme of love and eroticism, insofar as it is in this very split that the problem of repetition becomes essential. It is, in fact, through the feeling of love and its many forms that our existence appears in all its ambiguity, together with all that is both tragic and infinitely laughable in our lives. But what seems to be to be crucial in these novels which constitute so many tales of blighted love, is that he has been able to highlight the modern figure of repetition and desire par excellence: that of Don Juan caught in his turn in the trap of terminal paradoxes. It is the figure of a Don Juan pursuing his past tragic grandeur in vain and who scarcely has any choice left between the laughable career of a "curiosity collector" and the nostalgia of the idyllic Tristan.

Through its many Don Juans beyond the erotic pursuits of Martin or Havel, Tomas, Sabina or Rubens, Kundera's variation paints a picture of our entire modern culture torn between rationality and sentimentality. What Kundera reveals in double exposure, beyond each of his donjuanesque characters, is homo sentimentalis, the main subject of examination of all European culture in *Immortality*. His modern Don Juan pits his epic repetitions in vain against the lyrical fiction of an eternal return. Caught in such a vertigo of time, any tragic dimension escapes him and his very journey is transformed into so many grotesque acts of the tremendous comedy of double repetition. Caught up, without really knowing it, between the desire for a new catch and the nostalgic reminiscence of ecstasy held fast the eternity of time, he can hardly become anything other than a collector—of his own memories. His pursuit of knowledge itself becomes futile, for he knows from now on that a single repetition is sufficient to understand the uselessness of time and its deception. Through the wide range of repetitions where all the levels of composition and structure concur in a common Donjuanesque examination of time, Kundera achieves a fascinating novelistic synthesis in which the esthetic, erotic, ethical, playful and cognitive functions combine as in a single semantic river. If we think of Rubens, the latest of Kundera's Don Juans, whose desire can now only be roused by a nostalgic gaze fixed on a bygone past, we could no doubt call the river "Lethe."

The Eternal Return or a Dog's Happiness

In the journey, myth with its circular time, that of the eternal return as imagined by Nietzsche, logically becomes the object of choice of variational repetition. In *The Unbearable Lightness of Being*, a playful meditation on mythical time constantly crosses the path of human time which, for its part, does not repeat itself, but leads us in a straight line from birth to death. Kundera turns a skeptical look to the space where the paths cross, to the border between circular time and linear time. With ruthless lucidity, he here reveals the abyss separating our illusions and reality, between our desire for the idyll and the anthropological impossibility of its concrete realization, between the attraction of kitsch beauty and the unbearable irony of a beauty of knowledge.

Although it is true that the great European novels are love stories, if not stories of our illusions of love, beginning with those in Cervantes' Don Quixote, in Kundera's novels, the feeling of love becomes the main revelation of our entire imagological culture based on feeling elevated to a supreme value. Through the double exposure of the theme—between Tristan's love and donjuanesque eroticism—Kundera sketches not only the many virtualities and limits of our lives, but also those of the history of Europe. One of the strengths of his art in fact lies in this grasp of European culture as an existential situation based on feeling and in his capacity to reveal, through the window of the intimate, the various possibilities of that feeling.

In "Karenin's Smile," the final chapter of *The Unbearable Lightness of Being*, the nostalgic meditation on the impossibility for humanity of attaining the idyll and happiness as a desire for repetition, for the mythical eternal return, also reveals the most caustic irony in this great love story: the happiness of repetition and the smile of the idyll are here attainable—only by a dog.[19] In this fiction of the eternal return as a time of happiness and the idyll, Kundera once more suggests that all lyrical illusion, all deceitful masks of kitsch, in fact hide the very tragedy of our existence: our finiteness and death. Once does not count, once is never (*einmal ist keinmal*) and both history and human existence continue their unbroken fall forever, outside the circle of happiness where time is but eternal ecstasy. But throughout their fall, people notice in rare moments that they are dealing with illusion and continue to fall, filled with an unbearable sleepwalker's nostalgia for the paradise lost before the fall, and dream of being a dog.

Don Juan of Knowledge

"The Don Juan of knowledge: no philosopher, no poet has yet discovered him," Nietzsche wrote in *The Dawn of Day*. What was needed to succeed in this was no doubt knowledge specific to the novel. Thomas Mann's Don Juan in his magnificent *Doctor Faustus* is probably the first successful incarnation before the one we find in the journey of Kundera's Don Juan. Moreover, it seems significant to me that, in their journey to the past of European culture, Mann and Kundera, although in very different ways, both draw on the same source of musical variations, in this case Beethoven's Sonata opus 111. While Mann refers to it during the discussion between his Don Juan and the Devil, Kundera proceeds to explain the technique itself of his variation by analogy with that of Beethoven. In this way he himself raises the possibility of a poetic coincidence between the journey of his novelistic variations and that of donjuanesque knowledge. These two journeys rediscover endlessly, through their variational repetitions, inner time in all its dimensions and through this signal their disagreement with the absolute time of ecstasy, forgetting and death.

Ecstasy, the categorical agreement with present time, the total forgetting of the past and future, signals for Kundera the negation of time and the flight from chronology. Ecstasy, a time of forgetting par excellence, is at the opposite pole to the journey of knowledge of *all* the times which novelistic variation attempts in its exploration of the theme of love. In the final analysis, the donjuanesque journey does not in any way intend an escape from chronology, rather a playful deconstruction and reconstruction of it. The Don Juan figure, far from identifying itself with the "ersatz of eternity" as Kundera terms ecstasy, is certainly that of a Don Juan of knowledge. He is to be found both in Tomas in *The Unbearable Lightness of Being* and in Rubens in *Immortality*, to name but two. After all, do they not discover paradoxically, "there is no greater horror, no greater punishment, than turning a second into eternity, tearing someone out of the flow of time?" (IMM, p. 294).

The donjuanesque seductiveness of Kundera's writing traces above all an epic conquest and thus coincides with the account of his erotic conquest which, before being that of the female body, is that of language. Tomas, the epic (libertine) womanizer, does not have much of the lyricism (nor the intrinsic cruelty) of the idyllic loves of a Jaromil absorbed in the narcissistic quest for the image of his own self. Tomas, for his part, prefers to discover the millionth-part dissimilarity hidden in each of the women and which every time becomes for him a fragment of knowledge transmuted into language. I am thinking of his pleasure, a fundamental one for him, in grasping every erotic experience with words, through expressions which render epic his relationship with the other. But I am also thinking of the donjuanesque pursuit of Martin in *Laughable Loves* for whom the hunt for language (the desire for language) is already more important than the prey itself.

Although all Kundera's novels are beautiful stories of thwarted love, they are above all magnificent meditations on desire, understood in his work, as in that of Kierkegaard or Bataille, as an inner element of being. But this central figure of desire, like any object of Kundera's variation, will also be devastated by forgetting and filled with the strange, grotesque laughter which it generates. This desire, and Kundera's modern Don Juans are evidence of this, struggles in the paradoxical space of a border where the love of desire rubs shoulders with the desire for love, where the desire for illusion reveals, as in a double exposure, the illusions of the permanence of desire: behind Don Juan there always appears the figure of Tristan whose nostalgia reaches Don Juan. Conversely, behind the nostalgia for a lost paradise of idyllic purity of love and happiness the irony of a Don Juan breaks through, a Don Juan on whom his tragic destiny turns its back forever.

The End of Don Juan

Immortality, a synthesis of all Kundera's work, offers us one last cold look by the libertine to his past and, at the same time, to the past of European culture. The two facets of the donjuanesque journey—the narrative journey as well as that of the protagonists—come together. The paths of Don Juan's personal history and those of the cognitive journey of the Kundera's variations cross here and come to an end in their written form: the final gaze which Rubens casts on his past erotic quest retains nothing but a few fixed images (memory does not make films, it makes photographs! says the narrator) whose very memory already partakes of their forgetting. The semiology of seduction of his past life which he tries in vain to recall reveals to him at the end of the day that his entire quest for the knowledge of desire and existence was in fact, in its turn, merely an illusion: a "utopia of memory."

The invocation (that of Tomas, Sabina) of the lightness of time of a life which never returns (*einmal ist keinmal*), appears here in all its nostalgic beauty from which even the pleasure of counting innumerable conquests seems henceforth excluded. Looking to the past then becomes the sole recourse. But is desire not precisely, as Blanchot stated, the "ever-renewed infinite movement," the "repetition where everything which returns is nevertheless newer than any beginning?" In Kundera's work, eroticism appears to be the best path to point to the ungraspable void of death which has always hidden behind all repetition, be it variational or ecstatic. Between these two paradigms of repetition there extends the border of donjuanesque eroticism whose furthest poles represent both its stake and its impossibility.

Irony and Nostalgia

The figure of Don Juan appears in Kundera's latest novel as the very figure of its intrinsic structure, ambiguities and complexity. And more than ever before, the donjuanesque journey here points, by its repetitive crossings of borders, to the supreme cleft of time: the one between memory and forgetting and through this between irony and nostalgia. Should I pursue here the analogy between the end of the erotic quest and the possible end of the journey of Kundera's variation in its septenary form?

If "the art of the novel is the art of time and remembering," it proves to be truer than ever for the esthetic of Kundera's variation. But the novelist knows that remembering is not the negation of forgetting but one form of forgetting. It is therefore not a Proustian search for lost time for which he aims, but, to take up the title of one of the nine essays of *Testaments Betrayed*, the "search for the lost present," for the concrete moment, the only way we have of grasping reality knowledge of which is always deferred. Paradoxically, it is precisely this passion for the concrete which brings out in Kundera's work the nostalgic melody of an elusive time and which makes his work—and especially *Immortality*—one of the most beautiful meditations in novel form on the "fleetingness of time."

By virtue of its labyrinthine complexity, taken to extremes in *Immortality*, Kundera's novels are among the best of the late twentieth century insofar as they exacerbate, thanks to their double exposure of time, one of the fundamental characteristics of the age: the tension between irony and nostalgia. From the structure of his latest novel, one of maximum diffraction, and one which obeys more closely than ever the sole imperative of playfulness, comes the feeling of this nostalgia: the awareness of the possibility of the permanent loss of unity and totality as well as the awareness of a dissociation of the subject inscribed in all his characters. A loss which his variation in fact attempted to compensate by his seemingly infinite number of retellings and repetitions.

In Kundera's work, however, wherever nostalgia comes through, irony is never far away. Thanks to its perception of present time, the past (individual and historic) has a particular light shed on it. It becomes the privileged target of the variations and through this of its irony. Such treatment of time in fact characterizes the artistic production of our time where the road to the past leads necessarily to irony. This then becomes the only defence against nostalgia in the face of the irremediable fleetingness of time. And in fact, Kundera manages to remain on the fragile border where nostalgia and irony coexist thanks to the double exposure of time which he handles masterfully. In their reciprocal tension, nostalgia and irony reveal the very essence of Kundera's relationship to time as well as to the history of contemporary art that pervades his entire work. He thereby becomes not only one of the greatest novelists of the end of this century, but also one of the great figures of modern art as a whole.

The Fatality of the Number Seven

The number seven which in many respects marks Kundera's work, functions both as the figure of laughter and that of forgetting which emerge simultaneously from any quest for knowledge. The figure of septenary composition, it is also that of the art of combination, of the comedy of repetition and of the "theatre of memory," which extends a secret bridge between Kundera's esthetic and that of Fuentes of *Terra nostra* (a figure of chance, if there is such a thing) the only one able to summon, in the work of both writers, all the possibilities of time. *Immortality* contains all these possibilities: seven reveals itself both as a mark of lucid irony and nostalgic farewells.

Is it heretical to think that the donjuanesque journey, which is both the theme and compositional springboard of Kundera's novelistic variation, comes to an end with *Immortality*? That a formal configuration with the number seven at its centre closes? The idea of a comparison between the complexity of this novel and that of Mahler's Seventh Symphony haunts me. I am tempted to adjourn the present stay with Kundera with a poetic coincidence which I perceive between these two works marked by the encounter between the number seven and the colour blue, Novalis' motif of death which had once stigmatized, like a sign of farewell to life, other novels by Kundera, notably *The Farewell Party*. More than mere chance, it is his passion for the concrete which causes Kundera to specify that Mahler finished his Seventh Symphony in a hotel in Prague called *The Blue Star*. Kundera, for his part, also ends the composition of his seventh novel with blue: with the "beautiful blue dot" of forget-me-nots which Agnes had wanted to hold in front of her eyes before retiring permanently from a world submerged in the ugliness of ubiquitous kitsch, the blue on which she had wanted to fix her gaze, in order to summon from it, one last time, "a last, scarcely visible trace of beauty" (IMM, p. 345). Agnes, the imaginary self for whom Kundera shows a particular tenderness, was also born of a gesture of farewell, the sign of an infinite sadness in the face of beauty betrayed by time.

Chapter Two

Novel-Variation or Crossroads

> The whole journey, from the outline to the finished work, is made on one's knees.* — Vladimir Holan

> Only a slow reading, twice and many times over, can bring out all the ironic connections inside a novel, without which the novel remains uncomprehended.
> — Milan Kundera, *Testaments Betrayed*

Novel-variation, novel-path,[1] novel-questioning or novel-border, these are all metaphors which refer to the phenomenological essence of Kundera's novelistic esthetic. They invite readers to become in their turn "explorers of existence" and to take part in the simultaneously cognitive and playful adventure of the variations: there is "the abyss of the infinitely large and the abyss of the infinitely small. The voyage of variation leads into that other infinitude, into the infinite diversity of the interior world lying hidden in all things" (BLF, pp. 225-26). The voyage into the possibilities of human existence by means of experimental selves never takes a straight road, but takes random paths to which it constantly returns, thereby investing Kundera's novels with unparalleled narrative and compositional freedom. In touch with "the wisdom of the novel," my new journey through his work will consequently be mindful of the esthetic possibilities inscribed in the very form of his novels. I will therefore show that the beauty of Kundera's work in fact stems from the return to the past, from the collages of different times which are always lit in double

---

Notes to Chapter Two of Part Two are on pp. 132-34.

exposure: "Beauty is an abolition of chronology and a rebellion against time" (BLF, p. 73). Of course, this kind of reading is not without its pitfalls since each novel, and particularly *Immortality,* calls, in a quite exceptional way, not only on the readers' memory but also on their erudition. The journey proves to be even more difficult when we insist on reading Kundera's work as a single text, since we also have to rely on the memory of several textual surfaces and several (re)writings. There are innumerable themes and motifs circulating in his vast sum of knowledge, which is in a constant state of ferment, as well as formal elements belonging both to the most diverse domains of culture and to Kundera's impressive personal experience as a poet, musician, painter, musical and literary critic, not to mention his experience as "reader of philosophers" and that, no doubt less happy, as novelist "adapted" for the cinema.[2] Consequently, anybody believing that they could acquire the total memory of a "model reader" in such a textual maze, on the pretext of having followed the narrator of *Immortality*'s advice not to "skip a single line" of the novel, would inevitably hear a peal of laughter from Kundera's variations: laughter which knows that any "total" grasp of a work conceived as a crossroads of multiplicity is also the product of a utopia of memory. Even if Kundera writes "to retain memory," he knows full well, as do Jacques, Ludvik, Tamina or Rubens, that all rewriting is both writing and reading, and that it therefore does not elude the paradox of human time where memory exists only because of forgetting. When I read Kundera, I am haunted by a sentence from *Terra Nostra,* as if by a leitmotif: "Who am I? You are the one in memory. You are the other in forgetting."*

"Forward Is Anywhere"

In the vertiginous exploration of human and novelistic time, which reaches a climax in *Immortality,* a logic of causality or plausibility is of no help whatsoever. The only things which guide us are chance and an increasingly present narrator. The reader consequently feels thrown into a game of diabolo which the author-narrator constantly starts over again to prevent the reader from taking a character, story or speech (even his very own!) as *the* truth of the novel. The narrator holds out his distorting mirror to each of our vague impulses to consider narratives or characters as "real", showing them to be mere mystifying images behind which any illusion of plausibility vanishes irremediably. He takes malicious pleasure in interrupting our reading, repeating in a thousand and one ways that his characters are merely imaginary selves, born of a metaphor, idea or act, selves through which the author explores the possibilities he has not realized himself. He sweeps his reader into that border zone where not only what is and what was, but also what could be, are taken into account—the possible world of the novel. What is more, he constantly underlines his shameless fashion of scuttling the tense of the novel, he rewrites the story by borrowing a few new twists, composes freely using all tenses in order to make the paths of some characters cross with the paths of others. In short, he plays with the disparate tenses in the novelistic space with as much brilliance as he did in the "simultaneous dialogues" of his play *Jacques and His Master*.

It is up to his readers to construct an interpretive combination with their imagination, using their own fragments of memory, without forgetting however, that taking the crossroads which cut across Kundera's novels means rejecting, like the "minor seventh" which Jaroslav in *The Joke* likes so much, "the foolish scamper toward the key note with which everything ends, both song and life" (JOKE, p. 131). I shall therefore return once more to paths already trodden to follow Kundera's game with the form of the novel which, as one might well imagine, changes from one text to the other, upsetting along the way a few of the received ideas about the very limits of the *genre*. In the brilliant complexity of *Immortality*'s narrative syntax which the author-narrator wants to make programmatically impossible to relate and adapt, I hear once more Jacques' mystifying laughter before his master. Searching for the path and possible direction of their next adventure, both amorous and narrative, Jacques asks: "All right, then. I want you to lead me forward." The Master enquires: "Very well, but where is forward?" And Jacques replies "Let me tell you a great secret. One of mankind's oldest tricks. Forward is anywhere."

The Art of Composition

Kundera comments at length, in *The Art of the Novel*, on the three compositional principles of his novels: the art of ellipsis, the art of novelistic counterpoint and that of the specifically novelistic essay. It is the combining of these three principles, different in each of his novels, that drives the memory of the "four appeals" which allow Kundera to restore to the novel its continuity[3] and complexity, as well as to link the pleasure of the narrative game with that of reflection. Besides, when I speak of Kundera's "novel-variation" or "esthetic of variation" it is the combining of all the formal and semantic elements of his work that I mean by the terms, particularly the synthesis of his two poetic "techniques," variation and polyphony, which appear as the centre of the global structure of his work.

The Book of Laughter and Forgetting and *Immortality* explain, each in its own way, the compositional bias of Kundera's novels as a theme with variations. This does not mean that this principle regulates only the two novels cited, quite the contrary. In itself, the transposition of this compositional technique, at first glance a musical one, into the novel is certainly not new. But credit is due to Kundera for having made variational repetition the very basis of his entire questioning esthetic. It is a process, which, like the donjuanesque journey of a Tomas, seeks out a "one millionth-part dissimilarity" in each of its repetitions and which, to safeguard the lightness of the whole, summons up the art of the compressed turn of phrase, of ellipsis.

In undertaking its playful journey towards knowledge, Kundera's variation moves away from its theme to the point where "the initial theme, . . . resembles the last variation as little as a flower its image under a microscope" (BLF, p. 226). As a game, variation denies the very principle of realistic illusion and imposes on the theme a process of continuous change of meaning, thereby producing a new novelistic unit (thematic and not factual!) and, in the work as a whole, an astonishing network of intertextual resonances.

The Art of Ellipsis

Like the "Janacekian" imperative to strip one's style radically of ornamentation in composition, the art of ellipsis seeks the vital note to grasp "the complexity of existence in the modern world" (AN, p. 131). In Kundera's novels, that "note" is transformed into a few recurring "keywords" which reveal the existential code of his characters and which form the basis of the composition's thematic unity. Each of his novels rests in fact on very few such word-themes.[4] Paradoxically, they invest Kundera's work with an exceptional polysemy and formal diversity, and this is thanks to the very transformations which are imposed upon them simultaneously by variation and polyphony. Variation modifies them through the characters' numerous existential journeys, with the result that each narrative becomes a variation of the others; polyphony invests these same keywords with new meanings by examining them through a variety of discourses, with the result that the stories are not told in succession, but become enmeshed. What is more, Kundera's seven novels share a series of keywords which, like "cyclic cells," pass from one novel to the next in new metamorphoses, witnesses to the unity but also to the memory of the "thematic structure" of Kundera's work as a whole. Laughter, memory, forgetting, beauty, image, love, kitsch, border, or path are the best examples.

By using ellipsis, lightness of form is maintained and becomes all the more surprising as the variation plays with keywords of undoubted philosophical density. Take *The Unbearable Lightness of Being*: time, fortuity, necessity, love, death, betrayal, happiness, kitsch or weakness are simultaneously transformed through the different existential prisms and by discourses which everyone invests with a particular knowledge: erotic, political, musical, oneiric, philosophical, etymological, and so on.

The third part of *The Unbearable Lightness of Being*, with the significant title of "Misunderstood Words," represents without a doubt the most "condensed" form of the polysemic stakes in Kundera's art of ellipsis: a "short dictionary of misunderstood words," itself divided into three series, becomes enmeshed with the narrative of Franz and Sabina, thereby doubly underscoring the "abyss of semantic misunderstandings"upon which their love affair is based. What is more, certain words in this dictionary (beauty, betrayal, weakness) resonate throughout the entire novel as a mark of widespread misunderstanding and semantic imposture. In this way, for example, the word "weakness," linked in the "dictionary" to reflection on physical love, displays an entirely different meaning in Tereza's narrative and, through her, in the story of her occupied country.

But this "dictionary of misunderstood words" (fidelity, love, betrayal, beauty, weakness, music, etc.) itself restores language's lost ambiguity. What do these words mean? We think we know, we have our own truth concerning them, and yet, reading Kundera, that truth diffracts and breaks up into several relative truths and restores to each of the words its depth of polysemic possibilities. For Franz and Sabina, the same words mean diametrically opposed things, the two opposite meanings being both as true, as false, as the other.

It is as though each one of the key words resembled Sabina's "bowler hat":[5] "[it] was a bed through which each time Sabina saw another river flow, another semantic river: each time the same object would give rise to a new meaning, though all former meanings would resonate (like an echo, like a parade of echoes) together with the new one" (ULB, p. 88). Such is the case for the art of ellipsis for which Sabina's hat could well be a metaphor. In every one of these words, in every change of theme or motif and in every discourse which runs through them, Kundera brings out a new meaning which, as in a musical score, causes the meanings of the preceding and subsequent notes to resonate. In short, the art of ellipsis takes part in the overall recollective structure of Kundera's work like one of the defenses against "the forgetting of being" which only the questioning of the novel can grasp in its entirety.

The Polyphony of the Novel

The novel's ambition to be a sum of knowledge or gnosiologic synthesis of the Central European novelists, from whom Kundera claims decisively to draw inspiration, demands a particular economy of discourse. Rather than the term polyhistoricism which Broch uses in relation to such novels and which is far too "encyclopedic," Kundera prefers polyphony which is to be understood as writing composed of normally autonomous discourse, such as philosophical, historical, political, oneiric, erotic, etymological, poetic, scatological discourse, and so on. The aim of such polyphony is the maximum integration of these various discourses and their spheres of knowledge into the structure of a single novel. Kundera resorts to ellipsis precisely in order to preserve the architectonic lightness and balance of such narrative and discursive complexity. Without this supremely aphoristic skill, the complex network of narrative and discursive lines could not sustain the balance necessary to the unity of the novel and would risk extending beyond novelistic writing itself. Without ellipsis, without its "vital notes," playful meditation would risk slipping into purely philosophical reflection.[6]

However, Kundera, no more than Broch and Musil, for that matter, can only be termed a polyphonic novelist if we distinguish his particular economy of discourse from the "multiplicity of equipollent voices and consciousnesses," as Bakhtine defines them in his famous work on Dostoyevsky, or from the one practised, for example, in certain novels by Solzhenitsyn. The plan of the Central European novelists is both different and more complex. It is more complex insofar as philosophical reflection is integrated into the narrative and "reality" into dreams in one and the same contrapuntal movement, unlike the concept of "consciousness" itself. How can we speak of "equipollent consciousnesses" in Kundera's work when we know that his heroes are only the objects of their own mistakes and illusions, that they are only pseudo-consciousnesses which often take their particular point of view as *the* only truth of the story. The novel's "truth of the story" remains veiled to its protagonists. It appears in all its relativity and complexity only to the reader who is the only one who knows the overall structure of the novel. *The Joke* remains the clearest example in this regard insofar as none of the four narrators knows anything of the discourses of the three others, with the result that none of them will ever know the whole truth about Ludvik's story. The reader, on the other hand, can deduce the truth about the ironic confrontation of these discourses and thereby discover that the "truth" of all and sundry represents but one fragment in a vast mosaic of relative truths and knowledge, which polyphony in fact puts together. Furthermore, criticism of modern communication and language, which such discursive polyphony implies, can only be apprehended in Kundera's work from its overall structure and not through the consciousness of a particular subject at all, be it character or narrator.

The "Objectivized Subjectivity" of the Narrator

I am often surprised to hear so many readers who, although admirers of Kundera, reproach him for intervening in the narrative. Are they irritated in the same way by the narrator's libertinism in the works of Rabelais, Cervantes, Sterne and Diderot? It must be observed straight away that whether Kundera's narrator reveals to the reader the tricks of his formal technique, whether he selectively contradicts, completes or comments on the reflection of his characters or whether he takes up one of their existential themes in a specifically novelistic essay, he always maintains an ironic distance between himself and his imaginary selves as well as between himself and Milan Kundera, a biographical character. The voice of Kundera's narrator thereby deliberately abandons, if only by adopting an ironic tone in regard to himself, any notion of authority where "truth" is concerned and asks only to be a voice among many others in the novelistic scale.

The narrator's playfulness, as it is brought up to date in Kundera's novels, signals the end once and for all of the objective, anonymous and omniscient narrator, and also of the injunction which compels the author to withdraw as much as possible from his work. Kundera's narrator demands once more, and loudly, the forgotten pleasure of being a character in his own right, endowed with his own meditative subjectivity. That subjectivity must in no way be confused, and Kundera emphasizes this in countless ways, with the subjectivity of the narrator of a confessional text (autobiographies, private journals, etc.) in which the author reveals to the world the innermost secrets of the "uniqueness" of his own self, thereby acting more often in the spirit of graphomania of our times than the novel's spirit of irony. The "subjectivity" of Kundera's narrator can, on the contrary, be gauged from the ironic distance between his reflection and that of the characters,[7] but above all, and paradoxically, from the integration of his subjective reflection with the objective semantic structure of the novel.

Whether it is expressed through direct intervention in the narrative of a protagonist, or in the form of a specifically novelistic essay, each of his digressions remains linked contrapuntally to the "thematic structure" of the novel and, beyond, to that of all his novels. The narrator thus takes an active part in the playful and cognitive synthesis which constitutes the very essence of the esthetic of Kundera's variation.

Thanks to the ironic and contrapuntal structure of his novels, Kundera also cuts short any possibility of identifying his real biographical person with the author-narrator of his novels. For even when the latter is called "Milan Kundera," as he is in *The Book of Laughter and Forgetting* and in *Immortality*, we are obviously dealing with a character called Kundera. This is another way of exploring the author's narrative and existential possibilities, another way of mystifying his readers.. The end of *Immortality* remains the best example of this kind of mystification, a pleasure to which "realistic" novels that obey the imperative of verisimilitude have made us somewhat unaccustomed. In this way, the narrative scene of "The celebration" in which the author-narrator is transformed into a character who meets—and this is the epitome of quixotic coincidence—Laura and Paul, his own experimental characters, allows Kundera-author to have a role in his own novelistic game, while sending a veiled and mocking message to the reader. Especially to some "absolutely modern" reader who might be seeking (as Paul does) biographical rather than esthetic clues in the novel.

The Game of Polyphony and Variation[8]

The Joke and *The Book of Laughter and Forgetting* provide extreme examples of the synthetic game which Kundera brings into play between polyphony and variation to deconstruct the time of the novelistic story using different techniques in each of his seven novels. Let us begin with *The Joke*, which constitutes a special case in Kundera's novelistic creation insofar as it is the protagonists who share the narration. Each of the first six parts of the novel in fact belongs to only one of the four protagonist-narrators. Each of the narratives brings different points of view of the story of the joke experienced by Ludvik who thereby becomes the main character of the novel. But each of the four discourses belongs at the same time to another register of knowledge of which only the compositional construction provides the sum: Kostka's evangelo-mythic discourse occasionally resembles a sermon; Jaroslav's becomes a musicological essay; Helena's ideologico-sentimentalist and impossibly kitsch discourse contrasts with skeptical Ludvik's analytico-political discourse. In addition, in the seventh and last part of the novel, the polyphony is accentuated: Ludvik, Helena and Jaroslav share the narration in a crescendo where discontinuous narratives and intermingled voices are subject to a faster and faster narrative rhythm. The game with heterogeneous narrative and emotional rhythms which Kundera uses in all his novels takes the place, here as elsewhere, of the traditional dramatic crescendo of a linear plot.

In fact, in this novel, the narrative anticipates a much more subtle working which makes the "joke," as an element of plot, the object-theme of the variational transformations. It is a perfect example of the process which consists of enveloping rather than developing the plot, to use Musil's famous expression. The architectonic unity of the novel, referred to by critics as a "narrative symposium," certainly stems from the synthesis between polyphony and variation. In fact, the variation on the theme of the "joke" breaks up the progression of the story (and of history!) by unmasking it, with a burst of laughter, as a chronological and semantic imposture. It is one of the first experimental forms of Kundera's game with the time of the novelistic story and of the novel's "revenge" on history.

All the processes by which Kundera constructs his playful meditation on human existence—the juxtaposition of heterogeneous times and discourses, the intersection of narrative threads, thematic variation, the dispersal of linearity and causality—are mobilized in this novel. His art of ellipsis is also evident. In one single keyword, "joke," Kundera condenses his heroes' entire experience and, beneath that experience, the particularity of Central European knowledge: the individual and collective experience of history transformed into a "system of jokes," a system which has in its turn become the main object of the novel's derision. "What was it, then, that was mistaken?" Ludvik wonders towards the end of the novel. "History itself? History the divine, the rational? What if history plays jokes? And then I realized how powerless I was to revoke my own joke when throughout my life as a whole I was involved in a joke much more vast (all embracing for me) and utterly irrevocable" (JOKE, pp. 288-89).

Variation and Its Phenomenological Character

All the examples of how the esthetic of variation functions in the novel, with its synthesizing conjecture, both playful and cognitive, are good illustrations of the phenomenological character of this mode of exploring existence. This in no way means that Kundera's variation, even when it follows the path of critical or philosophical discourse, leads to, or results in, a system—quite the contrary. Moreover, Husserl's phenomenological thought remains above all open-ended. Its "eidetic reduction" also consists of an imaginary variation which reveals the essence of an object or a situation through multiple variations. This phenomenological mode of questioning man's identity which Kundera's novelistic variation pursues without respite, is certainly no stranger to his Central European spiritual experience. For there, even more than anywhere, people no longer recall their old values, no longer recognize themselves in their image, are no longer identical to themselves. Consequently, their selves split, their stories break up in a multiplicity of ways, their perspectives become many. It is therefore no coincidence that in a sociocultural context of this kind, affirmed by the First World War, there develops the novel's ambition to be a general gnoseological survey at variance with the crisis of European values observed by Husserl as well as Broch and Musil. "The Depreciated Legacy of Cervantes," the first chapter of *The Art of the Novel*, in fact begins significantly by recalling Husserl and his treatise on the "crisis of European humanity." However, while the cognitive course of Kundera's variation is directly in line with the extension of that experience, it is the playful and elliptical element which drives his journey of knowledge that allows Kundera to restore to the novel the humour and lightness of form which are so admired in the works of Sterne and Diderot.[9]

The phenomenological exploration of existence consists also of the protean repetition of a theme, a situation, a word. Everything appears to be the same and yet proves different every time, a game behind which is traced the playful logic of "repetition and difference." The development of the angel theme, which the narrator orchestrates in *The Book of Laughter and Forgetting*, strongly accentuates the phenomenological character of variation. In fact, the theme of the angels on the island where Tamina dies is preceded by a variation in part three of the novel. However, here again, the theme is transformed to the point of seeming to constitute its own negation: the story of the "angels," dominated in part six by the theme of forgetting, shows its reverse side, laughter, in the mirror of part three. Both are shaped by polyphony through several heterogeneous discourses. In this way variation reveals at the intersection of its various transformations the very essence of a situation or theme: its intrinsic plurality and ambiguity.

By undergoing new metamorphoses throughout its variational development, each of Kundera's themes is enriched with new meanings, to the point of being elevated from a simple thematic category to an existential or phenomenological metaphor, a term which Kundera uses in relation to Kafka in *Testaments Betrayed*. Such transitions from semantic category to phenomenological category throughout Kundera's work (think of the theme of the joke, laughter, border, kitsch, or path) allow the mixing of the individual and the collective which stems from the coexistence of different historical and individual times.

The development of the theme in a phenomenological (existential) metaphor through variational repetition can even be manifested by the recurrence of a single word, of which the "joke" remains the best example: at the moment when Ludvik thinks of the subjugation of his own joke to a "system of jokes," that of history itself, the word is repeated up to seven times in a single paragraph. In the name of such repetition, the "joke" can claim the status of a quite particular "phenomenological" category, that of a synthesis of knowledge which is specific to the novel and acquired throughout the textual journey. The new French translation of *The Joke* was therefore all the more necessary since, unlike the first one, it does not replace the keyword with equivalents: trick, fun, prank, hoax, game. Indeed, this unfortunate stylistic effort betrays the very basis of Kundera's variational esthetic: it debases the very theme of the joke to a mere decorative element of the plot, producing a mistranslation to boot, since it reduces the multiplicity of meanings which the theme acquires within the structure of the novel to an anodyne series of synonyms. The "synonymizing reflex" (p. 108) of many a translator, proclaims Kundera in *Testaments Betrayed* on the subject of Kafka's work, before exclaiming with him: "O ye translators, do not sodonymize us!" (p. 109).

Chopin's Strategy

Whereas in *The Joke* the work of polyphony might seem dominant, *The Book of Laughter and Forgetting* immediately establishes variation as the very principle of novelistic composition: it is a novel about Tamina, and whenever Tamina goes offstage, it is a novel for Tamina. She is its principal character and its principal audience, and all the other stories are variations on her own story and meet with her life as in a mirror" (BLF, p. 227).

When it was published, *The Book of Laughter and Forgetting* unleashed a polemic regarding the novel as a genre: can it be referred to as a novel when only parts four and six of the seven parts of the book are linked by the same character (Tamina), while the five other parts tell the story of different protagonists who are unknown to each other, who never meet and who have no factual link? Quite obviously, the coherence of the novel rests solely on the thematic unity, that is to say on a few word-themes which are shaped through different discourses and points of view. It follows that Tamina (unlike Ludvik) is the main character in *The Book of Laughter and Forgetting* only insofar as it is through her that the narrator, as the sole semiotic operator, best crystallizes the driving theme of the entire composition of the novel, the theme of forgetting.

That being said, this novel is neither the first nor the only one to be composed as a "serial repetition." *Laughable Loves*, as we know, is based on a markedly similar composition to that of *The Book of Laughter and Forgetting*. Accepted as a "collection of short stories," *Laughable Loves* does not raise any criticism of a generic nature. If we compare these two novels, their compositional parallelism (which Kundera himself emphasizes) seems obvious: part four and six in both works are also linked by the same character, Doctor Havel in the former and Tamina in the latter. In the same way as the latter, Doctor Havel also becomes the main character in the novel insofar as his existential theme, the split between love and eroticism, is the main aim of the game which all the other stories of "laughable loves" vary as they please. The central semantic category of the first novel, explained as always with Kundera by the title, becomes furthermore the privileged existential situation of the variational questioning in all Kundera's work. This also allows me to read it as a phenomenological exploration of European love. By inverting the perspective of my own reading, I notice that all the major themes and motifs which Kundera's variation take up and amplify, from one novel to the other, are already to be found, in embryonic form, in *Laughable Loves*. Laughter, memory, forgetting, beauty, border, identity, double exposure, donjuanesque games, and love, the speeding-up of the historical process, categorical agreement with being, image and identity, body and soul or shame and shamelessness, already outline in this novel the "structural thematic" of all Kundera's future work.

By integrating into the structure of the novel forms which are a priori not novelistic, in this case the short story, the composition of *Laughable Loves* and *The Book of Laughter and Forgetting*, allows Kundera to explore one of the esthetic possibilities of "redefining and expanding" the limits of the novel as a genre. In his essay *Testaments Betrayed*, Kundera specifies with regard to *The Book of Laughter and Forgetting*:

By giving each part the nature of a short story, I made unnecessary the whole seemingly unavoidable technique of large-scale novel composition. In my project I happened upon the old *Chopin strategy*, the strategy of *small-scale composition* that has no need of nonthematic passages. (Does that mean that the story is the small form of the novel? Yes. There is no ontological difference between story and novel, as there is between the novel and poetry or the novel and theatre). (TB, pp. 167-68)

The odds of (re)discovering a "novel form [of] almost boundless freedom" (AN, p. 83) which Kundera pursues programmatically from the first to last of his texts, are fully realized here: the composition itself of the novel represents the border on which heterogeneous and literary genres and discourses are equally established and through which knowledge follows the path of fortuity and imagination.

Furthermore, this freedom of form also allows Kundera to cross the border between the novel and other literary genres in the opposite direction: whereas *The Farewell Party*, the only novel composed in five and not seven parts, reads like a novelistic variation on the burlesque, the play *Jacques and His Master* is, on the contrary, a theatrical variation on the novel genre. Added to this, as I have already shown in speaking of *The Art of the Novel*, is the proximity between the semantics of Kundera's novels and those of his critical writings, a proximity to which *Immortality* and *Testaments Betrayed* testify admirably. All this allows me to read all Kundera's work as a great "homage to variation" as the most poetic mode of phenomenological exploration of existence possible and as the most capable of grasping being in all its intrinsic complexity and ambiguity.

Variations against Forgetting

In *The Book of Laughter and Forgetting*, Tamina's life, and, indirectly, that of all the other protagonists—but also the journey of the variation—boils down to a "struggle against forgetting." The Czech émigrée tries desperately to retrieve her late husband's "lost letters," because she believes that in this way she will be able to elude the forgetting which is gradually covering up her most private past. In vain she tries to recall the nicknames which her husband's tenderness once imagined for her and she cannot accept that "what she considered unforgettable could ever be forgotten" (BLF, p. 117). She clings to the "lost letters" as one clings to the hope of life. In vain too she practises a "special recollection technique of her own" which she has perfected and which consists of mentally remodelling, like the sketch for a painting, the face of a man seated opposite her to make it resemble the image of her husband, which is relentlessly being erased from her memory.

The adventure of forgetting experienced by Tamina in part four of the book undergoes in part six, entitled "The angels," a triple variation which takes the form of three stories stripped of all unity of action: the story of Tamina transported to the island over which the memoryless child-angels rule; Prague and Bohemia; the death of her aphasic father. The death sheds light in retrospect on what the father of the author-narrator had been trying to tell him about variation in Beethoven's music. The three stories, through their interlacing, simultaneously synthetize three forms of discourse (oneiric, historical and autobiographical) which in addition impart a polyphonic dimension to the novel. But this is not all, because variation, as we know, is characterized by the fact that motifs echo each other from one story to the other and weave a complex contrapuntal structure. So, for example, forgetting the endearments from Tamina's past love life corresponds to the forgetting which haunts Prague. Tamina's—and Kafka's—city becomes a "city without memory" where a vast "organized forgetting" erases the names of the streets, levels the culture of the people who inhabit it and eclipses the works which have emerged from it. The theme of "organized forgetting" continues on and reaches its height in *Immortality*: the imagological universe places the novel beyond history, beyond ideologies and even beyond memory, in a kingdom where people have already "forgotten forgetting," the forgetting of which *The Book of Laughter and Forgetting* was but an oneiric foreshadowing.

I am thinking, of course, of the forgetting which invades Tamina. The variation becomes oneiric and delivers probably one of the most terrifying of Kundera's visions of "organized forgetting" which is engulfing even language. Kundera situates the oneiric narrative (the word "nightmarish" would be more accurate) on a utopian island whose temporal status is, needless to say, indeterminate: it is simultaneously an island of the past, the present and the possible. This island, which, incidentally, has its counterpoint in the island of Daphnis and Chloe in the concluding part of the same novel, brings into play games which turn into a system that is both deadly and unvarying: without a past, without memory, forgetting is chanted in nursery rhymes devoid of meaning, expressed in language which obliterates Tamina's very name whereas she had desperately hoped to find her past names. What else but death could she have found, she whose body with an adult's memory becomes useless and even monstrous (her only name here is "tits") in this universe where time stands still in eternal ecstasy? She can hardly leave, because, in losing her name, she also loses her last link with humanity. I would like to call the story about Tamina "The departed" because, beyond the utopian world which marks Tamina's death, I continually perceive another utopia, as magnificent as it is premonitory: the phantasmagorical "Oklahoma theatre" of Kafka's first novel known by the title *America,* Tamina and Karl Rossman both become lost in the great theatres of "organized forgetting," whether they are called idyll, utopia or imagology; grotesque theatres, where people's names and identities are reduced solely to their function.

But let us return to Tamina whose existential theme, developed in parts four and six, undergoes new variations in the other parts of the book. Thus, Tamina's "lost letters" evoke the first part of the novel, also entitled "The lost letters" and where Mirek, another character, also tries to retrieve the love letters which he had once written to a girlfriend. But while Tamina's letters must serve (at least so she hopes) to reconstruct the language which has been dismantled by forgetting, those which Mirek is looking for are destined, on the contrary, to erase the past of which he is now ashamed. This reverse process, far from being limited with Kundera to an analogy accompanied by a mere substitution of characters, achieves the status of a veritable gnoseological exploration of the theme through its numerous semantic and formal, textual and intertextual transformations. The theme of forgetting, linked to graphomania and the love letters, for example, is taken up in new forms through the correspondence between Goethe and Bettina von Arnim in *Immortality*.

Playing with the Plot

The mnesic journey of variation in Kundera's novels takes on the appearance of a game with (versus) the tense of the narrative and does so even in the case of the *Farewell Party* although this novel rests on a strong plot. For Kundera, its themes are "worked out steadily within and by the story. Whenever a novel abandons its themes and settles for just telling the story, it goes flat" (AN p. 83). Of course the importance of the work far surpasses the simple matter of the story's interest. The esthetic value of the game stems in Kundera's work as much from the process of deconstruction and demythification of the novel's story as from its polymorphous nature. Taken to the extreme in *Immortality*, the game defies all the "conventions" which the reader might expect.

But what of *The Farewell Party* which is based on a formal archetype different from Kundera's other novels: "It is absolutely homogeneous, without digressions, on a single subject, narrated at the same tempo throughout, very theatrical, stylized, its structure drawn from farce" (AN, p. 93). And yet, we are not dealing here either with a causal and probable plot but with a farcical one, based on a network of motivic happenstances and quixotic coincidences as improbable as they are amusing. By toying with the "farcical tricks" of the plot, the novel destroys, in Kundera's words, "the verisimilitude pact" with the reader of the "realistic" novels and clearly revives the playfulness of the first period of the history of the European novel. The devices in Kundera's variation (the playful and the cognitive) find a perfect synthesis in this novel inasmuch as the work, which trifles with love as it does with death, is also an entertaining novel. "To bring together the extreme gravity of the question and the extreme lightness of the form—that has always been my ambition," states Kundera before emphasizing that beyond purely artistic ambition, he is aiming, above all, for the discovery of the human paradox: "The union of a frivolous form and a serious subject lays bare our dramas (those that occur in our beds as well as those we play out on the great stage of History) in all their terrible insignificance" (AN, p. 96).

Whereas Kafka enters the history of the novel through the "door of the farce" with *America* as Kundera suggests, he himself enters it through the same door with *Laughable Loves* and opens it in a pronounced fashion in the centre of his seven novelistic opuses: three novels in seven movements, one farcical novel in five movements and again three novels in seven movements. Is this a poetic coincidence, a hidden structure or an arithmetical passion? Whatever the case, I see in the farcical note of *The Farewell Party* the very "fold" of his entire novelistic score based on the figure seven, the centre par excellence of laughter and irony in the "human comedy of repetition" which his work presents.

Unlike his other novels *The Farewell Party* covers only five days which correspond to its five parts. The narrative tells the story of the pregnancy of Ruzena, a character around whom seven other protagonists gravitate and who are all connected to her by the developments of a handful of themes and motifs signaled explicitly by the problematic of repetition: love/procreation, life/death, fatherhood/motherhood, responsibility/irresponsibility, not to mention the theme of crime. All the characters without exception are confronted with the illusion of their free will on which the game of highly improbable coincidences sheds light like so many delusions of a "Lunar Adventure" which, moreover, is based on the motivic repetition of the colour blue, the harbinger of death (blue pill, blue nightdress, blue halo, etc.). Once again, only the reader knows all the tricks in the game of illusion and confusion, is the only one to know that the plot here is only a backdrop for pretence and upheaval where the farewell to death (Jakub who gets rid of the pill) in fact signals a farewell to life (Ruzena's). Life and death come together in "Ruzena's womb," Ruzena whose pregnancy, her "passport to the future" is in fact no more than a "masked death."

The narrative syntax of this both horrible and comic small masterpiece follows the spatial dislocation of the protagonists exactly as though it were a waltz, a dance in triple time. The entire narration seems to be based on the figure three which, as we know, destroys the polarity of the figure two and leads to the thematic exploration of plurality: three possibilities for getting rid of Ruzena, three topics of conversation between Klima and Bertlef, three reasons for nurse Ruzena's not liking people who take the waters, three men's eyes gazing at Ruzena, Kamila's afternoon with "three fauns," three suspects considered by the inspector, these are all signs of the complete breakup of the binary form. But, especially, there are the three bedrooms which the narrator highlights in turn like a stage where three couples are making love at the same time, in the same hotel, like a farewell in three variations, a farewell to life, to love, and to desire.

Discursive Time versus Narrative Time

In *Life Is Elsewhere*, the story of the novel consists of a "biography" of the poet Jaromil, related entirely in the third person. However, parts two and six of the novel destroy, each in their own way, the poet's "biography" by freely confounding narrative time and historical time. The narration of part two is attributed to Jaromil himself, whose "fantasy tale" about Xavier, his own imaginary self(!) opens an oneiric breach in the novel which explains all the subsequent schemes of the poet Jaromil like a series of highly ludicrous actions. Presented as Jaromil's attempt at a novel before becoming a poet, the surrealist narrative comprises three interlacing dreams about Xavier's freedom, dreams which represent as many ironic counterpoints to the actions of our lyric poet. The echo of the oneiric narrative resounds at point blank range in the final part of the novel where the dying Jaromil meets Xavier, his imaginary character. Kundera thereby clearly suggests that the life and death of the poet Jaromil are nothing but a laughable parody of his own lyrical dreams.

Part six of the novel cuts more radically into the plot of the novelistic story. The narrator "suspends" the narrative of Jaromil's death

("Do you hear the distant sound of Death, impatiently stamping its feet?" [LIFE, p. 270]) and transports his narrative "observatory" well beyond the poet's death. In so doing he opens up a "pause" in the story of the novel and a window into another possible novel, with an entirely new character, the forty-year-old hedonist. Kundera repeats the process in *Immortality* in which part six also introduces a new character into the story of the novel, Rubens, the last of his Don Juans. The compositional parallelism is all the more significant in that it introduces into these "novels within a novel" a donjuanesque character whose journey, following the example of the variation, reveals to the reader a new knowledge, a "millionth-part dissimilarity" of the novel's overall truth. Thanks to the "pause," the narrator explains indirectly what the narrative could not reveal: the veiled truth on the sex life of Jaromil's red-headed girlfriend in the first and on Agnes' sex life in the second of these novels.

In part six of *Life Is Elsewhere*, the narrator draws the reader's attention to the liberties he takes with the time of the novelistic story (liberties which neither the characters nor human beings can have) and to his new way of inverting the narrative perspective. However, the narrator plays not only with the temporal perspective, but also with the narrative rhythm, in such a way that the narrative "flows in a tempo opposite that of real life: the tempo slows down" (LIFE, p. 254), as though he were signalling to us that he will soon stop once and for all. It is as though the pause in the time of the story were emphasizing, through the moment of silence, that the plot is no more than a mechanism in a game which is far more important for the overall structure and meaning of the novel: variation's voyage inside the theme of lyricism. In fact, the novel's central theme is, in the donjuanesque chapter six, negated, both in the erotic and narrative meaning of the term.

I cannot leave *Life Is Elsewhere* without discussing the seventh and final chapter which, unlike Kundera's other novels, makes the death of the hero coincide with the end of the book. Does this mean that there is a happy end after all? A death worthy of the poet avid for uniqueness? No, no grand finale for Jaromil, because the novelist makes sure that other destinies follow the poet's death, providing a wonderful illustration of another possibility of his variational game with discursive time versus narrative time. Making as much use of elliptical technique as changes in narrative rhythm, Kundera brilliantly orchestrates a narrative collage of heterogeneous existential and historical times where an entire pleiad of European poets, all linked contrapuntally to Jaromil through the existential code of lyricism, coexist. Unlike time in Jaromil's life which becomes fixed in death, the discursive rhythm accelerates appreciably by revealing, in Jaromil's resultingly diminished death, his similarity with the European poets caught in the "trap of lyricism" (the trap of poetry, love and revolution) and whose journey comes to an end with Jaromil's: Jaromil is Lermontov, but he is also Pushkin, Byron, Shelley, Rimbaud, Mayakovsky, Wolker, or Halas all at once. His death thus reflects, like a shattered mirror of illusions, the entire history of European poetry grappling with the lyricism of reality.

In fact, the novelist achieves far more than mere "historical parallels" inscribed on the reverse of Jaromil's novelistic story, because the death of all the poets summoned to the final rendezvous literally implodes in the discourse, sometimes within the same sentence. This is an elliptical technique par excellence which transforms the story of Jaromil into a real existential metaphor of lyricism and emphasizes more than ever the reversal of all the values and situations whose secret Kundera holds: "A shot rang out, Lermontov clutched his chest, and Jaromil dropped to the icy concrete floor of the balcony. . . . In any case, there is nothing to stop us from changing the situation with a few strokes of the pen" (LIFE, p. 281), says the narrator in chapter twelve of the final part before ending it with a colon in order to underline graphically that the following chapter is nothing but its reversed image, the two forming a superb comedy of repetition: "A shot rings out, Jaromil clutches his chest, and Lermontov drops to the icy concrete of the balcony" (LIFE, p. 281). "The Poet Dies" and, meanwhile, the novelist lets out his peal of "devil's laughter" from within death itself : polyphonic laughter before the semantic imposture of all the lyrical masks which death assumes.

Multiple Focus

With *The Unbearable Lightness of Being*, the interplay between the themes and the story of the novel underlines in a new way Kundera's conception of the novel as a questioning of existence situated on the border between being and forgetting, memory and forgetting, being and non-being, lightness and heaviness, shit and kitsch, an epic attitude and lyrical temptation. The journeys of the four main protagonists do not form any linear plot but rather the sketch of a painting in a constant state of ferment where, as Scarpetta writes, "a calculated intertwining of semi-dependent plot lines" which correspond neither to the points of view of different narrative authorities (*The Joke*), nor to the reflexive technique of independent stories connected by one and the same theme (*Book of Laughter and Forgetting*). As Guy Scarpetta emphasizes, this novel is based on a "technique of multiple focus [which] allows the time of the discourse to be shifted in relation to the time of the story"*: the first and fifth movements focus on Tomas, the second, fourth and seventh on Tereza, while the third and sixth focus on Sabina and Franz.[10] The multiple focus hardly allows one to speak of "main character," because the narrative threads of this amorous quartet are in balance in the overall structure of the narrative. I would add, however, that chapter seven focuses as much on Tereza as on her dog Karenin whose structural importance is even foreshadowed by the title: "Karenin's Smile." Karenin figures here as the ironic vanishing point of the entire structural thematic in the temporal paradox explored in the novel: he is the only "character" capable of offering Tereza an idyll, the only one to escape the unbearable duality of body and soul, the only one who does not seek his image in the mirror. This animal idyll, outside human time, fills the last part of the novel with a strange sadness made more acute by the fact that Kundera's readers, for their part, have known since part three that Tereza and Tomas are dead. And as Tereza's dream reveals, the sadness assumes that we know.

In the Labyrinth of the Novel

With its programmatic fragmentation and maximal diffraction, the structure of *Immortality* cannot be reduced to any standard categorization. The author-narrator guides us more than ever through the very process of his composition where three narrative threads of heterogeneous times intermingle, literally fighting over the border between reality and fiction, between life and the novel. *Immortality* is, among all Kundera's novels, but also among all the European novels of this century, without a doubt the one which most redefines and expands the idea itself of the novel as a genre. It dispenses conclusively with plot and dramatic tension, which is referred to as the worst curse of the novel as genre. The story of the novel-border does not only open up to the times of its experimental characters, but also to the age-old story of European culture (viewed also as an existential situation of love) which takes up as much space in the narration as Agnes' narrative and that of Goethe. Whereas *The Farewell Party*, to give an extreme counter-example, takes place over only five days, *Immortality* covers two hundred years of history, even allowing itself digressions as far back as the thirteenth century (in part four entitled "Homo Sentimentalis," the longest and most beautiful "specifically novelistic essay" of all Kundera's work), all the digressions being perfectly blended into the structural thematic of the whole. The two "historical" parts (second and fourth) are inserted between the odd-numbered parts of three narrative threads about Agnes, the central imaginary self of the novel, some parts being connected to others by a vast range of themes and motifs which cut through the various narrative and discursive movements. Part six, as we know, is a "novel within a novel" which, by introducing a new character (Rubens), sheds light "from outside" on Agnes' existence as examined by the three narrative threads which the novel devotes to her.

Unlike the very broad temporal structure of the novel, the seventh and last part covers no more than an hour. However, it is an hour in which the times of the author, the narrator, the reader and the characters are also summoned to a final narrative encounter of downright farcical improbability. It is as though the author-narrator, whose work no one any longer reads, (not even his friend professor Avenarius!), were making a final attempt to raise laughter from the border between life and the novel before the latter becomes completely unrecognizable, a mere "dimensionless dot" outside history. Composed in five acts, the final part contains certain similarities with both the composition of the "Symposium" in *Laughable Loves* and the one in *The Farewell Party*. This discreet sign indicates once more that the novel (and its author-narrator) leave the stage of his novelistic score in seven opuses by the "door of farce," in exactly the same way he entered.

The composition of *Immortality* explicitly defies Aristotle's law of causal chain which excludes any minor event from the narrative framework. Rather, the playful logic of Kundera's variation makes use of all the possibilities that "produce stories" hidden in every episode which, consequently, forms a part of the development of the novel's structure. Agnes, the main heroine of the narrative thread taken up in three parts of the novel, becomes, viewed from the erotic and narrative perspective of Rubens, a "woman-episode" (IMM, p. 306) whose significance is echoed in the overall structure of the novel.

"For How Long Can a Man Be Considered Identical to Himself?"

Touching on countless themes, discourses and destinies, the journey of variation breaks the rules of determinism of the novelistic story, just as it breaks the rule of history which is also viewed, and I emphasize this, as an existential situation and not as a "background" of fiction.

Such a playful process constantly weaves the central phenomenological metaphor of all Kundera's novels: that of questioning man's identity, an identity which is irremediably fragmenting while allowing the individual self to disappear behind the images imposed on it by the fashion of the day.

For how long can a man be considered identical to himself? Kundera wonders in *Testaments Betrayed*, a question which drives all his work (TB, p. 213). The existential metaphor of schizoid dissociation between the self and the image of the self in *Immortality* actually represents the last phase of a long intertextual development whose initial variations are to be found as early as *Laughable Loves*. "The Hitch-hiking Game" is an excellent example: erotic role-playing transforms tender love into a cruel parody of love and the modest face of a young girl into an shameless image of a loose woman. When the role-playing finally ends, the heroine desperately repeats in vain the tautological "I am me, I am me, I am me," her soul remains hidden for a long time by the image imposed on her by her lover. The narrator does not really say whether the young man recalls, nor after how much time, the face of the young girl he loved for her shame. But the reader has learnt during this episode (the lovers forsake the route they had planned for their holiday journey in order to follow a path at random) that it is difficult to maintain the status quo between one's identity and the image which is constantly imposed on us from outside. Humanity imposes "faces" on itself, said Gombrowicz, and his skeptical sniggering in the face of the immaturity of people unable to cohere with their own image sharpens the irony of Kundera's variations on the same theme. Agnes in *Immortality*, full of the knowledge supplied to her by the journey of variation of all Kundera's previous novels, can no longer dream of anything but a world in which there would be no faces, a world in which people would compose their own image. In the distance, beyond his sad, silent dream, I can hear the sarcastic laugh of Ferdydurke who also knew that "man depends on the picture of himself formed in the minds of others, even if the others are half-wits."[11] Let me repeat that it is no coincidence that part one of *Immortality* is entitled "The Face" because behind each face we constantly find another one and realize that the one we thought was "real" was in fact only a facade or, in the words of the novel, an image of the self. This novel thus emphasizes more than ever that we are experiencing the complete fragmentation, or even extinction, of individuality.

Moreover, the figure of Agnes frequently crosses the border between the first-person narration (the narrator's time) and the time of the narrative related in the third person, thereby rendering even the border between the two narrative "faces" barely discernible. The whole thing is emphasized by motivic repetitions which bind the different characters and times together: "the gesture of longing for immortality" made by Bettina von Arnim, by Agnes' father's secretary, by Agnes, and by her sister Laura, not forgetting Paul who reduces the gesture to a mere caricature; or the motif of the "dark glasses" which also links Agnes' time to Goethe's, and so on. These motifs forge secret links among the different figures, often allowing them appear as variations of each other.

With *Immortality*, we find ourselves more than ever before crossing temporal, narrative and discursive borders, together with the further ironic addition of the time of the immortals. The impossibly grotesque posthumous encounter between Goethe and Hemingway evokes to a degree another famous literary encounter between immortals, that of Vivaldi and Montezuma on Stravinsky's grave in Alejo Carpentier's *Baroque Concerto*. In *Immortality*, Goethe and Hemingway converse merrily, although not without bitter irony, on the immortality of their work. But such immortality also proves, in its turn, to be nothing more than a mask hiding their new posthumous death since people are no longer interested in their work, but in the more or less spicy moments of their "biography." Even this slight interest on the part of posterity in the authors' lives actually conceals another imposture since their so-called biography reduces their life to the image which posterity has deigned to leave, a kitsch image par excellence since it conveys value judgements and received ideas on the author rather than esthetic knowledge of the work. What is more, this posthumous time finds a variation in a caustic specifically novelistic essay on the "eternal trial" which Rainer Maria Rilke, Romain Rolland and Paul Éluard conducted against Goethe not because of his work nor even his life, but because of the false image given to it by Bettina in the obliterating rewriting of their letters.

Although it is true that the narrator's meditative part is more extensive in the composition of *Immortality*, it is nevertheless perfectly balanced with the other narrative threads, while dispensing entirely with the plot. From that point of view, of all the novelists of this century who have taken the formal experimentation the furthest with a novel conceived as an instrument of knowledge and truth, Kundera deserves a choice spot inasmuch as he has pushed the negation of the plot to the limit, while still continuing to tell stories. *Immortality* thus represents the most successful experimental possibility of the composition of a novel seeking to maintain the balance between fiction and reflection.

The Kingdom Where Time Stood Still

The imagological world explored in *Immortality*, situated beyond history, is based entirely on kitsch as the art of forgetting par excellence, the immutable time of happiness and the idyll. The novel can therefore be read as an extreme variation of all those variations which, throughout Kundera's work, explore the various facets of all categorical agreement with being whose esthetic ideal is kitsch. However, in *Immortality*, kitsch is examined in the age of imagology, the kingdom which disposes of all conflictual reality for the benefit of beautiful images to which everyone adheres to escape the passing of time, and little do they care that the images are only compensatory. In the world of imagology, it is even forbidden to disagree with others, an interdiction which seems superfluous since nearly everyone aspires only to conform to the latest image fabricated by the imagologues, with the result that kitsch ceases to pose a threat since it is in agreement with the "pleasure" of the greatest number.

The world of imagology and narcissism par excellence of this novel becomes at the same time one of legalized voyeurism: ubiquitous cameras reduce even the most personal memory to a few images served up to the public.[12] At the end of the novel, on the edge of the swimming pool where the author-narrator meets Paul, his character, the latter speaks and his image is infinitely diminished by the mirrors which entirely cover the walls. Here, a mirror ceases to be a place where an imaginary subject is created and becomes, on the contrary, the place where it disappears: the play of the mirrors' surfaces (in both the literal and metaphorical sense of the term) no longer reflects anything but the images of the self like so many enticing masks of institutionalized kitsch. But what is most important, from the formal point of view of the novel, is that this imagological society transforms any "questioning" communication characteristic of our "society of the novel" into imagological communication or, to use Baudrillard's term, an "ecstasy of communication."[13] In fact, as we already know, ecstasy for Kundera signals the complete forgetting of human time, and along with it, the forgetting of being. All this is not without repercussions, as we might expect, on the structure of a novel which persists in pursuing its questioning of existence in a world of ready-made answers and which in its turn stubbornly refuses to become an image outside history, in frozen time where both laughter and desire are emptied of all memory. This is precisely why what is needed is a new way of writing novels which are not relatable and adaptable, an esthetic and ethical intent in which Kundera is very clear.

What can the novel conceived, as an infinite questioning of existence, do in a universe of ready-made answers where even death is concealed by the ubiquitous din of kitsch?" It can seek silence for death in order to offer a last refuge to beauty and shame, as Agnes and her father wish. In fact, at the very heart of such an exclusively imagological world, Kundera succeeds in letting a note of silence be heard by inserting twice—first in translation, then in the original German—"the unbearable nostalgia" of a poem on death written by Goethe which Agnes has learned to love thanks to her father. The poem thus becomes one of the motifs of memory linking the two temporally heterogeneous narrative threads of the novel, Agnes' time and that of Goethe. Together they hint at the final note of desire for beauty arising from the encounter between two different eras. But the motif comprises in addition the memory of previous texts since it also lets the echo be heard of death-beauty of which the narrator spoke in *The Book of Laughter and Forgetting* in relation to a short story by Thomas Mann. It lets the faint note of a "golden ring falling into a silver basin" be heard in order for silence to emerge: "He needed that silence to make beauty audible (because the death he was speaking of was death-beauty), and for beauty to be perceptible, it needs a minimal degree of silence" (BLF, pp. 143-44).

Uniting the Impossible

Behind all the many techniques, of which I have touched on only a few, there appears the novel as a form of ontological questioning which abruptly reveals the essence of human existence in all its ambiguity. Kundera's novel works as a synthetic "playful meditation" which looks at specific human situations from many standpoints of knowledge: dreams, analysis, narrative, etymological, philological and autobiographical discourse, and many others. Even by comparing *The Joke* and *The Book of Laughter and Forgetting*, I was able to see that history itself represents in his work only one novelistic element among many and that it is neither more important nor less laughable than the others (the history of Stalinism or the Prague Spring is as ludicrous in character as the personal history of Mirek, Jaromil or Tomas).

However, beyond existence, Kundera constantly questions the formal possibilities of the novel, and the novel is also examined as an existential situation, which once again clearly demonstrates that the novelist remains a reflective novelist from beginning to end. And all the more so as his characters are in equal measure products of the exploration of a word, situation or metaphor, allowing us to see them through their existential code rather than through physical or psychological descriptions, or even less, through an "interior monologue." His protagonists, every bit as much as the narrator, are thus inextricably linked to the variational development, like so many contrapuntal possibilities of a given series of themes. It follows that certain characters appear to attentive readers, as I have indicated, as a variation of those they have already met in another novel by Kundera. The long line of his Don Juans (from Doctor Havel or Martin to Tomas, Eva, Sabina or Rubens) no doubt remains the most striking example. But one can also think, to give another example, which is just as significant as it is conflicting, of the variations of the lyrical series which forges intertextual links between someone like Jaromil in *Life Is Elsewhere* and Bettina in *Immortality*, to cite only these two great graphomanic figures in Kundera's work.

Furthermore, through the frequent development of the concrete in the life of his experimental characters from an abstract idea, Kundera manages at the same time to grasp the code of their era, even their anthropological essence. He himself observes that, through the heroes he scrutinizes in the age of terminal paradoxes who herald the end of the modern era, the possibility of an actual end to the suprapersonal history of certain European adventures can be foreseen: "the grotesque fulfilment of European poetry" (AN, p. 40) in the figure of the poet Jaromil, the end of libertine adventure through Rubens or, as the journey of Tamina, Tereza or Agnes suggests, the abandoning of the very road of humanity.

Life and the novel: two existential situations which both resemble "a composition that musicians call *a theme with variations*" (IMM, p. 275). The comparison emphasizes as much the self-reflecting construction of Kundera's variations as its intertextual value. It seems significant to me that Kundera speaks in *Immortality* of "existential mathematics" because, if I may extend the metaphor, the structure of the novel evokes analogies with fractals which suppose that the smallest new fragment, the smallest motivic development added by a variation, possesses the characteristics of the whole and vice versa. The "structural thematic" of all his work is based on the same principle since each of his seven novels, each semantic path traced by his variation from one novel to the other, minor as it may be, always supposes the memory of the other texts.

The meaning of a novel conceived as a game, as a mnesic journey of knowledge, can hardly be deduced from the ending. For "to want to deduce the meaning of the ending, as Patocka writes, is to subordinate it to the category of causality,"[*14] a category which any phenomenological questioning of existence actually challenges. In that sense, Kundera's novelistic variation, with its erratic jaunts, paths and episodes, remains the mode of poetic exploration most appropriate to the "total"grasp of a world which is falling apart. The journey of the variation constitutes thus the best metaphor for desiring the knowledge of human existence. A metaphor which effects "condensing of meanings through a series of displacements" and which, "showing culture in actuality,"[*15] is in categorical disagreement with all the metaphors of affirmation and decorative embellishment, which I would like to call the imagological metaphors of kitsch.

Searching for the "Border"

I have demonstrated many times how the voyage of variation as a metaphor of knowledge and memory is composed, from the outset, of the exploration of a border on which coexist opposite and contradictory meanings of discourses, situations, themes or words, with the result that such a metaphorical border is vital in Kundera's work as the space of ambiguity par excellence and, thus, as the iconic centre of the novel.

The border, the title of the last chapter of *The Book of Laughter and Forgetting*, becomes a conspicuous theme elevated, what is more, to an existential category of repetition. What is this "border?" It is the place where things lose their meaning. In other words, novelistic variation is an uninterrupted phenomenological investigation of the metaphorical border on which things still simultaneously possess and no longer possess their meaning. An unusual sign is often enough to indicate that the border has been crossed and provoke laughter, the "Devil's evil laughter" of the novel and variation. Sometimes even a cubist perception of a face "on the borderline between the repellent and the attractive" (*The Joke* does so for Helen's face), a mere reflection in a mirror is enough to see the other face of love transformed into "ridiculous acts" (*The Book of Laughter and Forgetting, Laughable Loves, The Farewell Party*, etc.), or merely a hat set down by the wind, like an unusual sight in the gravity of a burial service, is enough to provoke the laughter of the Devil and the novel in a solemnly funereal crowd (*The Book of Laughter and Forgetting*).

In fact, the consciousness of the border, ubiquitous from the first to last of Kundera's books, is specific in its conception of the novel in general: his novel never affirms but questions indefinitely the uncertainties and the absolute relativity of things. In his work, the border represents the absolute character of that relativity. In the imagological society of *Immortality*, we in fact witness the disappearance of that border and, logically, the disappearance of that which constitutes the very specificity of the European novel: laughter, irony and humour. "Humour can only exist when people are still capable of recognizing some border between the important and the unimportant. And nowadays, that border has become unrecognizable" (IMM, p. 332). Is it surprising then that this novel should push to the limit the exploration of the metaphorical border between memory and forgetting, laughter and forgetting or between desire and forgetting, but especially between the novel and life? It is on this border that the history of the European novel bears an overwhelming resemblance to the time of individuals and that, with their disappearance, the novel as it was created at the dawn of the modern era would itself cease to exist. Thus, the disappearance of this border in *Immortality* evokes not only the possibility of the end itself of the libertine journey of Kundera's variation, but also the possibility of the end of "the spiritual identity of Europe" as a society of the novel.

Part Three

Don Juan's Final Glance, or the Memory of Desire

Half the history of the world at least is, indeed, a love affair! Of course, that is counting every kind of love!*

— Robert Musil

The vast panorama of history depicts the course of our species through the no less vast catalogue of ideals, which attests both to their appeal and to their inadequacy; from a certain angle then, does not the whole of history inherit from it a certain donjuanesque attitude?*

— Ortega y Gassett

After my previous explorations of Kundera's work, it is more than tempting to return to the paths of love which crisscross the length and breadth of the European novel and which Kundera's novels recall. Such a journey would cover many forms of love and desire, from platonic love to unemotional eroticism, from "true love" to "beyond the border of love," beginning with Cervantes' *Don Quixote* and ending with Kundera's *Immortality*. But then it would be a question of a "voyage inside the time of Europe" entirely different from that which I am making in the company of Kundera's variation, of an entirely different book to come. Consequently, in my most recent exploration of his novelistic score of recollection, far from depicting the innumerable situations of love and desire which characterize it from beginning to end, I have followed only a few of the scattered paths in search of Europe's inner time, in search of the secret border where desire decides between memory and forgetting, life and the novel, the donjuanesque conquest of the narrative and the epic adventure of a Don Juan struggling with the lyricizing of love.

The figure of Don Juan emerges from my preceding explorations of Kundera's work as a structural figure of the double textual journey, both scriptural and erotic, although his actual erotic adventures are not addressed. This is why, in this final exploration of his work, I am anxious to examine the innumerable existential possibilities of love (of

Notes to Part Three are on p. 134.

"all kinds of love"!) compared with the figure of Don Juan. This allows me to shed a singularly clear light on the bridge which the novelist extends beyond the entire history of modern culture (of love, the novel, painting, music) by depicting desire as the most ambiguous and exacerbated form of human time, of its illusions and—repetitions.

Indeed, the inevitability of repetition reaches its captivating height in the exploration of the division between the semantics of love and those of eroticism, the essential situation of all his experimental characters on the point of desire. It is probably on this polymorphous stage of love that Kundera no doubt disturbs his readers the most insofar as love becomes the privileged object of merciless demystification of our remaining illusions on free will. The novelist speaks of the choices we make in love as so many products of lyrical nostalgia for "lost unity," for an idyllic time filled with dreams of universal harmony and illusory (but terribly reassuring!) images of a "world without conflict," in other words of nostalgia for a tranquil time untroubled by the fleetingness of desire. The echo of that nostalgia sounds in a variety of ways in all the love stories questioned by Kundera's variation, in the form of archetypal images whose attraction comes from our collective unconscious and from which no one, Don Juan any more than Tristan, seems to escape. In fact, as Kundera never ceases to remind us, from the first to last of his novels, "they aren't our stories at all, . . . they are foisted upon us from somewhere outside" (LL, p. 34).

From *Laughable Loves* to *Immortality*, the donjuanesque voyage of Kundera's variations into the existential possibilities of love and desire remain closely linked to the exploration of our identity and, consequently, of our individual and historical memory. In fact the novelist himself makes clear that the "erotic stage" remains for him a privileged place where all the themes of history reveal their innermost secrets, for they have not yet, at least in theory, been publicly revealed there. He is thinking, needless to say, of secrets forgotten by historiographers and which only a knowledge of the novel can reveal, on condition that it does not seek to illustrate a particular historical situation, but rather examine, through love, "the historical dimension of human existence" (AN, p. 36). Thus, beyond the personal time of his characters, his phenomenological questioning of love reveals the existential code of the entire history of modern culture. In this regard, *Immortality* alone justifies a "voyage inside the time of Europe," insofar as the theme of love and eroticism inscribed in the text draws on the major modern works of literature.

Memory of Desire

Kundera never describes a love story, any more than his numerous scenes of coitus, simply to embellish a novelistic framework wanting in drama. His questioning of love in all its forms is always thoughtful, with the result that his variations lead to the greatest knowledge of both individual and historical time, a privileged path to restore some fragments of memory to "the forgetting of being." By exploring the possibilities of love in this age of terminal paradoxes and by comparing them with those of the past, Kundera is more aware than ever of the need to safeguard memory and continuity:

> The speed of history has reached such a point that the link with the past is at risk of being broken. This confronts the novelist with a fairly new task: to save continuity which is being lost, capture the fleeting time of history and indirectly place in parallel our way of living (of feeling, of thinking, of loving) and that, half forgotten, of our predecessors.[*1]

Kundera's particular ironic genius in fact stems from his art of variation, the art of paradox if ever there was one, for he maintains historical continuity of love through the figure of breaking-up and discontinuity par excellence: the figure of Don Juan, in fact. The double inclusion of his donjuanesque questioning of time, which is both a principle of writing and a thematic goal, creates a fascinating synthesis of the novel where, as we have seen many times, the esthetic, ethical, erotic and historical functions combine in a single existential flow. In Kundera's chronicle, the very word love is clarified by new meanings with each variation, like a mirror placed between memory and forgetting, between knowledge and illusion. This allows Kundera to make us see love as an oxymoron, for even the desire of his Don Juan, also caught in the trap of time, is slowly supplanted by the desire of Tristan, the most famous figure of homo sentimentalis.

Don Juan's Journey

Far be it for me to pick out at this point the thousand and one musical or literary faces of the famous womanizer, to retrace his age-old and infinitely varied journey since his appearance. I shall merely recall that throughout the four centuries of his mythical existence, a time which coincides significantly with the four centuries of the European novel's history, the figure has undergone as many metamorphoses as the form of the novel itself, by destroying all order, both social and novelistic. A particular imaginary space is created around Don Juan, one which holds a favorite mirror to each of the periods he explores, to his questionings on desire in its relationship to time and repetition. Through the proliferation of his conquests inspired by the desire for a constantly deferred elsewhere, which is infinitely more important than the true possession of a woman, Don Juan becomes the revelation of desire as a temporal form of transgression and repetition. It is, however, a repetition whose metaphysical truth reveals our anthropological illusions, those which place us on the border between our inescapable mortality and the permanent seductiveness of the mirage of the timeless.

From his tragic greatness in Tirso de Molina's play, where, as a man of transgressions, he pays for his inability to love with his life, to the baroque figure caught in a constant vertigo of being and seeming, hiding his face under countless masks and disguises, he always plays on desire confined between the moment and duration. Similarly with Mozart's Don Juan who, nevertheless, plays on the tension between the tragic and the comic, or with the romantic figures whose desire lives on as the quintessence of all desires whose fulfilment remains suspended by eternal renewals. Contemporary metamorphoses of Don Juan explore in numerous ways the contradictions of the character and reveal, with great irony, his ambiguity more than his tragic dimension.

A victim of his own seductive ploys to which his prey now surrender without the resistance which once filled his conquests with sensual pleasure, the modern Don Juan is relentlessly retreating from his initial tragic fate. His very game of seduction often proves useless, because the initial deploying of his seductive strategies and the actual catch have become so dizzyingly close that nothing remains for him but to enjoy the narcissistic (and somewhat pathetic!) satisfaction of his own language rather than the objects of his desires. Of the great conqueror there remains all too often but a smooth talker who juggles with pretty little phrases in order to produce the calculated effect on modern-day beauties. Thus, from the rebel and man of transgressions that he once was, he reluctantly becomes a mere conformist in agreement with the *Zeitgeist*. That spirit is signalled with Kundera, as we have often seen, by ubiquitous kitsch, with the result that, to continue as an effectual seducer, Don Juan must, in his turn, as Kundera says so well, "play on kitsch." In short, he is more of a casual user of women or a Casanova than a seducer, more of a collector than a conqueror, and his journey from now on has a comic edge, a border which Kundera reveals with as much irony as he does brilliance.

Take Martin in "The Golden Apple of Eternal Desire," the first of Kundera's Don Juans, who has just turned forty and whose pursuit of women amounts to a game of flirting: a game where "it had become less a matter of women and much more a matter of the pursuit itself" (LL, p. 59), because his wife, as much loved as she is feared, waits for him at home for a game of cards. Trapped, like Doctor Havel or Tomas between a double desire, his erotic journey is transformed into an "absolute pursuit," a touching "self-deluding game" which pushes the "the knight obsessed by necessity" into territory which has neither love nor love affairs. His infinite possibilities for eroticism remain sublimated, perceptibly changing the desire of this strange Don Juan into Tristan's love. Of the great conquest there remains for Martin but a game obeying very abstract rules which impose themselves on him like necessity and immutable worth, and which reduce his "conquest" to banal and laughable stages of "registration" and "making contact" in the street. Thus, right from the beginning, the journey of Kundera's Don Juan is to be found on the border between fortuity and necessity, a paradoxical space if ever there was one, where Martin, Havel, Jan, Tomas and Rubens, to name but these, are so many variations.

Between Fortuity and Necessity

Whereas Denis de Rougemont in *L'amour et l'Occident* also defines Don Juan as Tristan's absolute opposite, Kundera, on the other hand, shows the two figures of desire in double exposure in their disturbing proximity and interchangeability. He never shows them in a binary and dialectic relationship, but in coexistence, on the very border of the ambiguity to which the novel, as the art of time and the complex, can give the best form. The novelist, better than a historian, philosopher or sociologist ever could, captures the twentieth-century drama of love and eroticism and, thus, our crisis of identity, showing both its seriousness and its incredibly comical aspect at the same time. In his lengthy phenomenological questioning of love, Kundera carries out the project described in *The Art of the Novel*: he sheds light simultaneously on the comic aspect of history and sexuality. Through his existential metaphor of European love of which the modern Don Juan (and not Tristan!) becomes the central revelation, Kundera's variation constantly points to the rational facade of our culture as being a false setting which conceals, to use the words of the narrator of *Immortality*, the real "engine of history" in the West: homo sentimentalis.

I am thinking of Tomas, the doctor of ars erotica who, in a dream, meets the ideal woman for whom he has been searching all his life and yet decides to follow his Tereza, the "woman born of six laughable fortuities." Tomas knows that the "woman from his dream was the 'Es *muss sein'* of his love" (ULB, p. 238), the lost half of the myth of Plato's *Symposium*. He also knows that "love is the longing for the half of ourselves we have lost," a desire for unity and fusion, and that people never meet their lost halves. And even if one day his dream were to come true, a single "infinitely sad expression in [Tereza's] eyes" would be enough to make him abandon for her sake, defeated by compassion, the paradise of necessity with the ideal woman. The compassionate love which he drags around all his life like a weight, will get the better even of his donjuanesque quest, which, before being a quest for female bodies, is a quest for knowledge. By comparing the woman in his dream with Tereza, Tomas suddenly understands that any game of necessity is nothing but an impossible dream, an unrealizable utopia.

Why then Tomas' strange sadness at the end of his life? Might he have come to understand that the choice of fortuity over necessity which he made after long hesitation does not stem from his free will either? For does not the appeal which has arisen from his unconscious in the form of a metaphor change the fortuity of his love for Tereza into necessity? Tomas' ultimate knowledge has certain similarities with the "mystical period" of Rubens' erotic consciousness, when the latter suddenly understands that all erotic images come from "an impersonal stream" which does not belong to us but rather to the one who created us (IMM, p. 280). With Kundera this signals the definitive end of any illusion concerning free will in love. Rubens' knowledge can be viewed as a negative variation of Tomas' assertion that excitement belongs to the realm of necessity (which therefore belongs to the "mechanism our Creator uses for His own amusement") and that his love born of fortuity is his only freedom (ULB, p. 236). But no one escapes altogether, Tomas any more than you and I, if only for the duration of a dream, from that nostalgia for lost unity which nurtures our hopes as well as our disappointments in love. Being no exception, Tomas, the Don Juan famous throughout Prague for his some two hundred conquests, will have only to dream of a new utopia—in short, an erotic Paradise—where his love for Tereza will be rid of the "aggressive stupidity of sexuality," a dream which, ironically, definitely places him outside the time of human eroticism.

Don Juan in a Tangle

Kundera's entire semantics of love are thus linked explicitly to time, squeezed between memory and forgetting, between remembering and its negation. It struggles between necessity-fate and the non-fate of fortuities, in a journey where, together, the limits of our existences are inscribed and played out. But I want to repeat that what Kundera is interested in are not these extremes in themselves, but the exploration of the border zone which unites them and which draws from their paradoxical juncture a polyphonic beauty of new knowledge where I often seem to hear the echo of Nietzsche's words calling necessity "fate" while knowing that fate is never the abolition but the combining of all fortuities.

Kundera's exploration of the paradoxical space between an unemotional eroticism and emotional love underscores more than ever the game and the stakes of the double repetition (of a double desire) which drives all his work. What is the act itself of love if not a series of repetitions ad infinitum in which Don Juan, whether his name be Tomas, Jan or Rubens, plays at being the master of difference. And is the dream of uniqueness and idyllic happiness of someone like Tereza, which conflicts a priori with donjuanesque desire, not also defined as a "desire for repetition?" And yet there is no possible comparison between these two modes of repetition, between, on one hand, the ironic donjuanesque journey and, on the other, the circularity of an idyllic world driven by the nostalgia for paradise lost. Kundera combines these two forms of repetition: even his Don Juans "of knowledge" know that they can hardly escape time and death, any more than they can entirely elude the lyrical nostalgia of repetitious sameness. In the final analysis, their own mirror only reflects back to them the image of the exhaustion of their own desire and points, through this, as in a two-way mirror, to the possibility of the end itself of eroticism.

Desire in the Time of "Terminal Paradoxes"

In the world of terminal paradoxes where the imperative of feeling silences all questioning and knowledge, received ideas are substituted for love, and contrived gestures, as imitative as they are laughable, for eroticism. What becomes of the lucid gaze of the libertine in such a universe? What happens to the unfeeling desire of the legendary Don Juan as well as to the feeling desire of the no less famous Tristan, the two mythical figures which continually impress themselves on our imaginations? Does Don Juan still make use of irony and Tristan of nostalgia? Nothing, as one might suspect, seems less certain in Kundera's novels. Beyond the "all kinds of love" which his variations depict from one novel to the next, a scaled-down Don Juan emerges from as many oxymoronic figures where love and eroticism, sexuality and the gratuitousness of erotic pleasure mingle and are superimposed. The pleasures of the flesh and the pleasures of language are united and allow the desire for love to be mirrored in the desire for desire, the desire for illusion in the illusions on the permanence of desire. The many figures of donjuanesque eroticism emerge from the very cleft of time and its fleetingness; they are inscribed in a double repetition which is both mnesic and ecstatic.

Whereas, for Broch, eroticism acts as a bridge out of solitude, in Kundera's work it becomes, on the contrary, a revelation. Kundera suggests that words can act as mere substitutes for physical contact. The game of linguistic "register and make contact," a game emptied of desire for any carnal exchange known to Martin, is continued in *The Unbearable Lightness of Being.* Unlike Martin, Tomas comes to possess some two hundred women's bodies, and yet, he only records, in the end, a few brief linguistic formulae, because his "poetic memory" is literally occupied by his Tereza. Words sometimes serve not only as substitutes for the sexual act, but also as a mirror for physical love. For Jan in *The Book of Laughter and Forgetting,* words become the only meeting of the bodies of his partners in erotic games, whereas with Edwige he makes love while remaining amazingly silent. It is the same with Rubens in *Immortality* whose act of love often comes, it will be remembered, from language itself.

The Anthropological Trap

With Kundera, Don Juan's course thus opens up a paradoxical space divided between an epic journey and constant lyrical temptation, between the constant desire to pursue a multitude of women and, simultaneously, the temptation of one single, even fusional, love. From Doctor Havel or Martin in *Laughable Loves,* to Rubens in *Immortality,* including the forty-year-old in *Life Is Elsewhere,* Jan in *The Book of Laughter and Forgetting* or Klima, Jakub and Bertlef in *The Farewell Party,* and of course not forgetting Tomas in *The Unbearable Lightness of Being,* they are all caught, in varying degrees, in the trap of one single anthropological dilemma: that of too fine a borderline joining eroticism to sexuality, erotic games to the necessity for procreation as well as the inaccessible idyll of feeling to the gratuitousness of the unfeeling erotic game. As Kundera states in relation to the forty-year-old in *Life Is Elsewhere,* the "desire to reconcile erotic adventure and idyll is the very essence of hedonism—and the reason why it is impossible" (AN, p. 132).

Kundera's Don Juans all remain more or less entangled in a snare of this double desire: caught between the pursuit of dissimilarity and the idyllic search for uniqueness, between the desire for knowledge of the other and pre-knowledge "desire for desire." By fusing the two legendary figures of Don Juan and Tristan, Kundera presents a "hybrid" type of Don Juan who now bears only the name of the man in the street (Havel, Martin, Tomas or simply the forty-year-old, and who are all, incidentally, over forty!). Tomas in *The Unbearable Lightness of Being* becomes an explicit example of the double face: through the figure of Don Juan there constantly appears, as if behind a fake set, that of Tristan: beyond the epic womanizer who relentlessly pursues the "millionth-part dissimilarity," in a multitude of women, there emerges the lyrical lover overwhelmed with compassion for Tereza's sufferings.

Through the explicit double exposure of Don Juan and Tristan in one and the same character, Kundera underlines more than ever the similarity between their reciprocal illusions. Starting from two entirely contradictory attitudes towards love, their desire, by different paths, vainly pursues the same goal: that of escaping the clutches of passing time forever. The Don Juan side of Tomas will vainly raise the ramparts of his epic and differentiating repetitions against the lyrical fiction of an eternal desire for sameness. Caught increasingly between what he thought was his destiny and an unbearable nostalgia for the love born of a biblical metaphor and "six laughable fortuities," he finally gives up his pursuit of women and dies, as Tristan, by Tereza's side. Does Kundera not once again suggest that, in place of "free will" which we had hoped to exercise at least in love, we find in the end only another illusion, whether it is part of necessity or fortuity? After all, what sort of freedom of choice can be found in a love which, like Tomas', would not have happened without his head of department's sciatica, or like Jacques', who, had he not fallen from his horse, would never have fallen in love?

The Tragedy of Desire

To play an epic stance against a lyrical stance through two womanizers and two types of desire also means, with Kundera, playing donjuanism against kitsch. Broch had seen the danger of kitsch in the "conspiracy of monogamous puritanism against the Enlightenment" and the distinction which Kundera explains, in *The Unbearable Lightness of Being*, between both types of desire confirms the thinking of his illustrious predecessor. Pitting the "lyrical womanizer" against the "epic womanizer," entails distinguishing between, on one hand, the pursuit of the same subjective ideal of *the* woman cast onto all women (Franz, Paul) and, on the other, the pursuit of difference in each of them, of which Tomas and Rubens are perfect portrayals. In Kundera's typology, the libertine womanizer is associated provocatively with the "misogynist" who is identified as the only one able truly to love a woman, while the romantic womanizer, as a perfect "worshiper" of femininity, prefers her to the knowledge of a real woman. This division between the two types of desire foreshadows the variation which Kundera creates in *Immortality* between "love-relation" and "love-feeling."

It seems significant to me, in view of the double desire of which I have just spoken, that in the rich panoply of Kundera's Don Juans, none of them is able to withstand the nostalgia of the love idyll. It is in fact only the forty-year-old Sabina and Rubens who continue their solitary (albeit post-monogamous experience) journey of erotic "betrayals" until their own desire is satisfied. Sabina seems to be, from this point of view, Kundera's most liberated character; in fact, is this not because her code of existence is based on "betrayal" which, as Bataille writes, is the very truth of eroticism?[2] Indeed, to the very end of her life Sabina refuses to let herself be enslaved by love, which, for the overwhelming majority of Kundera's characters, including his most celebrated Don Juans (Martin, Doctor Havel, Tomas) becomes literally occupied territory. As for Agnes, when she finally decides to "slam the door" in the face of love's illusion, in both the literal and figurative sense, it is already too late.

The Duality of the Erotic Relationship

Through the many love affairs, donjuanesque or otherwise, a clear line is drawn between licit sexuality and eroticism. For Kundera, and for Bataille, "human sexual activity is not necessarily erotic. It *is* erotic each time it is not crude, each time it is not merely instinctive."[3] With Kundera, however, eroticism is not based on climax, transgression or pain: "Not pleasure or climax or emotion or passion. Excitement is the basis of eroticism, its deepest enigma, its key term" (AN, p. 128).

Excitement in fact becomes, throughout Kundera's work, something which is shared between erotic desire and the desire for love, or, in Tomas' words, between the desire to make love with a large number of women and the desire to sleep beside just one. As for Sabina, who in this regard resembles Johannides in Kierkegaard's *Diary of a Seducer*, likes, as a consummate artist of erotic performances, to look at herself in the mirror making love with Tomas. She observes intently the excitement where body, bowler hat, physical strength and scatological imagination together forge a privileged erotic moment. With Franz, on the other hand, the repetition of the same scene shifts the moment into the realm of the comic, beyond all excitement. With her sentence "love means renouncing strength" and by feeding their erotic secret to his wife (in the name of respect for *woman*), Franz unwittingly excludes himself forever from Sabina's erotic life. Unlike Sabina, Tereza believes that the excitement of the body comes from that of the soul, and her desire to become Tomas' "only body" pushes her imperceptibly beyond the border of her husband's erotic quests. It is in fact another way of exploring the duality between body and soul, a duality which finds a new variation in *Immortality*: here excitement separates two diametrically opposed attitudes in the face of the love of the two sisters; while for Laura the body is always sexual, for Agnes, the woman-episode of Rubens' eroticism, the body in fact only becomes "sexual" at the moment of excitement.

Through his playful meditation on excitement, Kundera's narrator thus explores in a somewhat heretical fashion the very Christian separation between body and soul: he also gives us a glimpse, as if in passing, of time in which the body suddenly becomes aroused by the betrayal of its soul, if I may put it thus. It is Tereza excited by the idea of the only occasion she was unfaithful to Tomas during her coitus with the engineer, a betrayal which is, above all, as "episodic" and brief as it can be, a betrayal of her own idyllic imagery of monogamous ecstasy; or Agnes excited by her body seen in a mirror between two men, a moment where no "will to love" as she describes her love for her husband, comes into it. If betrayal is in fact the truth of eroticism, it takes on in these scenes its entire transgressive dimension in relation to straightforward sexuality. How can we not also think of the cry Tereza lets out on her first coitus with Tomas, the first and last cry of their entire married life! The cry is not one of climax or excitement, but a cry of ecstasy which, on the contrary, wants to silence her senses, to forget the unacceptable duality between her body and soul. The cry is all the more revealing in that it responds, in a cruel paradox, to her other cry, a sensual one in this case, the one which results from her brief coitus with the engineer, a coitus from which she nevertheless emerges with immense disgust. But as we are reminded by the narrator, who on many occasions meditates on the memory of desire, the "memory of revulsion" is stronger than the "memory of tenderness" Tamina in *The Book of Laughter and Forgetting* had long known something about that.

Love and Power

Yet, in *The Farewell Party*, which deals with nothing but love stories, couples and couplings, excitement and eroticism are virtually absent. Here all the love relationships develop where the prevailing mood is far more one of desire for power over the other than of carnal desire. Furthermore, love is overshadowed by reproductive sexuality, whose potential for power and manipulation is also shown. The farcical plot of the novel unfolds in a small spa town where sterility is treated. There are a vast number of women and very few men. "By the time she reaches fifteen [a woman born here] is likely to have a perfectly clear picture of all the amorous possibilities life is likely to offer her" (FP, p. 29). The comic aspect of sexuality becomes unbearable, especially during the last night when the coitus of the three couples (in which the three men are nevertheless regarded as Don Juans: Jakub, Klima and Bertlef) appear, in varying degrees, as so many negations of eroticism, without much spark of erotic excitement. Jakub makes love to his ward Olga, out of a sort of paternal duty. Klima remains constrained before Kamila, his "scandalously beautiful" and adored spouse, as if on "an operating table" where he could no doubt not get a hard-on even at the sight of a swallow if Tomas' dream were to come true. The idealized love for his wife, which he takes pleasure in calling his "erotic secret," can only lead to failure as it rests above all on the paralyzing fear that she will discover his infidelities.

There is only Bertlef, the sensual and devout sixty-year-old Don Juan—the only Christian in the tradition of Kundera's Don Juans—who seems to be an exception. For him, as for the ageing Doctor Havel in *Laughable Loves*, eroticism is not only "a desire for the body," but also "a desire for honour" (LL, p. 94). Paradoxically, he is the one who allows the pregnant Ruzena (a pregnancy which, for Klima, at once pushes her into the "asexual territory of fear"), to experience a dazzling moment of erotic magic. But the miraculous moment rapidly blends much more with a cloud of death heralded by a bluish light than with desire and excitement.

The "Desire for Desire"

A metaphor for a libertine outlook which is both scriptural and erotic, Kundera's Don Juan, as a denier of all univocality, tries desperately to remain on the border of sexual ambiguity without which eroticism can barely survive. Jan in *The Book of Laughter and Forgetting* knows that it takes so very little to topple over the borderline, where the very body

movements of love are turned into ridiculous gestures, into a "stereo-
typed gesticulation," into a mimetic repetition devoid of sensuality or
excitement. In the hilarious scene of the collective orgy organized by
Barbara, the sex "Field Marshall" who directs the sexual activities of
her guests as though it were a party meeting, Jan suddenly realizes
that the gestures of the bald man who is making love on the other side
of the room resemble his own, exactly as if he were watching his own
reflection in a mirror. The gazes of the two men at this point have only
to meet to make them break into helpless laughter, which, as might be
expected, the organizer of the orgasmic festivities cannot forgive. Their
laughter resounds in the novel and echoes the laughter of Tamina
when faced with a champion of orgasm, who, like a goal scorer on a
soccer field, quantifies his life's ecstatic adventures on television, with
a seriousness worthy of the greatest agelasts: "If an orgasm lasts five
seconds, I have had twenty-five thousand seconds of orgasm. That
makes a total of six hours and fifty-six minutes of orgasm. Not bad,
eh?" (BLF, p. 135).

Realizing that he lives in an age of orgasmic accountancy and cli-
max without excitement, in short, an erotic simulacrum, Jan then
begins to dream of Daphnis and Chloe, to desire desire: "He desired the
pounding of the heart. He desired to be lying beside Chloe unaware of
fleshly love. To transform himself into pure arousal, the mysterious,
the incomprehensible and miraculous arousal of a man before a
woman's body" (BLF, p. 311). Does Rubens in *Immortality*, at the end
of his long erotic journey, not feel the same thing? While making love
to his latest conquest, the beautiful Australian student of "the semiol-
ogy of painting" (and who would no doubt have done better to study
the "semiology of coitus" first, as the narrator suggests with his
fabled impertinence), Rubens realizes that he is only performing "vac-
uous motions, and he realized for the first time that he didn't have any
idea why he was doing it" (IMM, p. 309). And for the first time, both
Jan and Rubens wish to return to the past which is now being lost in
forgetting. Jan wants to go "back to man's beginnings, to his own
beginnings, to love's beginnings" (BLF, p. 311), to the beginnings of
desire. In other words, Jan begins to desire an erotic idyll, aware that
he desires the impossible.

During his most recent lovemaking, Rubens is no longer able to
grasp the meaning of the word "love" with which his young partner
punctuates the conversation. Does the word refer to the act of physical
love or to the feeling of love? He is obsessed by the idea to the point
that he begins to have "breaks," as must, he thinks, the professor

of semiology of painting with his partner of the inelegant (and limp-making) runners. Without desire, eroticism loses all meaning and Rubens, just as in Jan's case, feels a "strong, tormenting nostalgia for the women of his past" (IMM, p. 310), nostalgia for his own erotic past. He knows from now on that, without excitement, he will no longer be able to experience new desires, that he will be able to turn only to the failing memory of his past desires. If the author-narrator speaks of Rubens as "the saddest erotic story" he has ever written, it is no doubt because the memory of desire on which his donjuanesque journey counted so much, was only, in its turn, an illusion, a final utopia.

Martin, Havel, Jan or Rubens appear in Kundera's work as so many revelations of the exhaustion of desire in an age which, never-theless, prides itself on being one of sexual liberation. They all find themselves facing the same nostalgia for a desire which is dead and gone. "When you go with everyone you stop believing that such a com-monplace thing as making love can have any real meaning for you" (LL, p. 94). Consequently, for Doctor Havel as for all his subsequent variations, the legendary desire of the "Great Conqueror" that was Don Juan (and from whom a single look was worth "ten years of the most unremitting physical love"), is lost in forgetting. In the world of the "Great Collector," eroticism is no longer worth anything more than a meal or a game of ping pong because, as Doctor Havel states with sad irony, the collector has let "eroticism into the ordinary round of events" (LL, p. 111) for good. By making the sphere of death into the "realm of death" in this way, the modern Don Juan replaces the con-quest of the impossible with the accessible where the tragic Don Juan is nothing but a distant memory. Like the lucid Doctor Havel, Kun-dera's Don Juans (and, with them, the "postmodern" Don Juans of our cities) could exclaim in a single voice: "Not at all, Madam, I am at most a figure of comedy." And even their "comic sadness" (LL, p. 112) falls to them, as again Havel understands, thanks only to the memory of the myth of Don Juan without whom their life of common "woman-izing" would be nothing but "grey banality."

The Comic Aspect of Sexuality

It is the comic aspect of sexuality of which Kundera's Don Juans are conscious. A sacrilege! would no doubt exclaim the Jaromils, Bettinas and other agelasts from the heights of their "planet of inexperience." By revealing the comic aspect of his Don Juans, the novelist, with much irony, imperceptibly shifts seduction and eroticism over to the territory of love-kitsch: to the "kingdom of the heart" to be found, unlike the initial donjuanesque journey, "beyond joking," beyond laughter, in the kingdom where it is not love but received ideas about the feeling of love which guide his conquests. I am thinking especially of Helena, Jaromil, Ruzena, or the student of the "Litost" in *The Book of Laughter and Forgetting* and, of course, of Bettina von Arnim. Poets and lyrical lovers, as we have known since *Laughable Loves*, all join with the ideological and imagological agelasts in the same hatred of laughter and irony. The novelist's playful logic makes all these lyrical bipeds and enemies of laughter the privileged target of his novelistic irony and subversion. Jaromil doubtless remains the best example of this insofar as, I have stated repeatedly, his amorous lyricism, a mixture of immaturity, innocence and cruelty, blends wonderfully with that of the age in which he lives.

Even coitus is not spared Kundera's laughter and even becomes one of the privileged scenes of the comic aspect of sexuality: the supposedly erotic act is transformed into an athletic exercise where love is often conspicuous by its absence, with the result that beds resemble a great chess board. Consider the resentment of the student of *litost* after his night of love—with no coitus!—with Christine, at the moment he realizes (when it is too late) his own absurdity: "Casting his eyes into the unfathomable depths of his stupidity, he wanted to burst into laughter, into whimpering, hysterical laughter" (BLF, p. 205), the laughter, I would add, of *litost*. However, fortunately for the student, poetry flies to the rescue of the lyrical and disappointed lover—in the guise of a note from Christine in this case—and prevents any devilish temptation to laugh. Failing love he still has poetry. "Nothing but poetry," is the narrator's ironic retort with regard to "the bungled story" of the student who is not even able to find consolation in the comforting memory of coitus.

Among the Don Juans of knowledge, Jan, Tomas and Rubens are without a doubt the most aware of the fine borderline separating eroticism and sexuality from laughter, the insidious trap of lyrical loves, both individual and collective. They all know, as Jan knows, that only "a few millimetres separated [them] from the other side of the border, where things no longer have meaning" (BLF, p. 292) and that, once it is crossed, "fateful laughter rings out." When we give ourselves over to laughter, as Jan does at Barbara's, we run the risk of seeing desire disappear as if by magic. This seems to be even more true when we are dealing with organized and (pre:) programmed sexuality and where, straightaway, any erotic relationship fails miserably. Laughter, the Devil's, needless to say, is what, with Kundera, connects the vision of sexuality with that of history, a connection whose unacceptably comic aspect, Kundera, with irony tinged with sadness, reveals.

"The Gesture of Desire for Immortality"

Unlike the epic womanizers, Kundera's lyrical womanizers have usurped and kitschified desire be letting it simmer in the great "samovar of feelings" in the words of the narrator of *Immortality*, with the result that for them, the criterion of absolute love can only be measured by the rod of death. Fleischman in "The Colloquium" is one of the first examples of which Helena, Jaromil, Laura, Bettina and many others are so many variations. They have all replaced the memory of desire (for a real man or woman) by a pathetic and comical desire for immortality which in fact signals the negation of desire.

Driven by the feeling of her failed love, Laura "wants to do something." She dreams of committing pathetic suicide (how similar she is at that moment to Helena in *The Joke*!) in the house of her scoundrel of a lover. Through this act she wants her body to remain eternally engraved on his memory. This is surely more effectual revenge than the slap given by the student in the narrative "Litost" to his girlfriend who had the misfortune to be a faster swimmer than he. The gesture of immortality by Laura who, for her part, already stands "beyond history," in an imagological world, can only be elevated in a laughable act of charity, that of collecting money in the subway for lepers in Africa. The gesture of desire for immortality in fact disguises the emptiness of desire by replacing it with the "struggle" for immortality, that "pathetic illusion" of remaining engraved in the memory of one's nearest and dearest (minor immortality) or in that of history (major immortality).

Unlike Laura and her posthistoric world, Bettina von Arnim can still live the grand "gesture of longing for immortality" of which Laura is now but an imitator. However, even if, for Bettina, history represents "eternal memory" (IMM, p. 164), her act connecting "the absolute of the self" to "the absolute of the world" does not contain any more room for love than Laura's since, as the narrator emphasizes, any real individuals who find themselves between these two extreme poles are immediately excluded from the game. Desire for immortality—now there's a feeling that salves the narcissistic wounds of a soul which, by transforming it into an gesture, becomes a "hypertrophy of the soul," the one which *Immortality* signals as the real engine of minor, as well as major, history: that of homo sentimentalis, that of Europe. This is an unhappy displacement of desire which Kundera examines on the many forms of love's stage with bitter irony which some could no doubt forgive.

On Procreation

Another favourite border explored by Kundera's variations signals to the temporal fracture between eroticism and procreation, a border over which Kundera's Don Juans keep a fearful eye. Procreation for them has also to do with the first categorical agreement with being which, as we know, forms the very basis of kitsch with Kundera. According to *The Art of the Novel*, a libertine can only be happy with a woman he loves who has no children, or with many women. It is therefore not surprising to see them all build a dream where love and procreation are dissociated. Whereas for Jacques, the worst end to a love affair is a "brat," for Jakub, "parenthood implies absolute affirmation of human life" (FP, p. 91), with the result that he dreams of "liberating love from procreation" while his friend, Doctor Skreta, wants "to liberate procreation from love." By joyously injecting his sperm into his patients who yearn for children, Doctor Skreta is on the point of realizing his private totalitarian utopia, where everyone would be brother and sister, in a perfectly mimetic repetition. The children of his little town already all have a nose resembling the famous doctor's, a nose which marks them forever (and without their knowing it) with a comic poignancy.

The Last Temptation of Christ

Among Kundera's Don Juans, there is however a notable exception to the general refusal to have children. The very Christian Bertlef, certain of the agreement he would obtain from Jesus for his love of women (of many women!), is as an indirect result in perfect agreement with God's creation, and therefore with procreation. Indeed, the sixty-year-old Don Juan, whose life hangs by a thread because of a serious heart disease, does not in any way dissociate procreation from love and even interprets the arrival of a child as a perfect expression of the unforeseen. His young wife has just given birth to a son and Bertlef awaits their arrival by staving off his impatience with a night of love with Ruzena who, as we already know, also represents for him a link between eroticism and procreation!

Is this then the fulfilment of our Christian Don Juan's last procreative temptation? Do we at last have a Kunderian Don Juan in "categorical agreement with being!?" Such thinking would betray ignorance of Kundera, who, in this small masterpiece of burlesque, mystifies his characters as well as his readers in his usual wonderful fashion. As a joyful mystifier who sold his soul to the devil of laughter some thirty years ago, the novelist suddenly displaces the unforeseen by which Bertlef believed he had fulfilled his last temptation of the agreement with God's creation, by including it in a superb comedy of repetition: the Bertlef's newborn, unbeknown to the happy parents, is of course (we might have guessed!) the biological son of Doctor Skreta who—and this is the height of comedy—has meanwhile become Bertlef's adoptive son and therefore the brother of his own son. A comic holy trinity reunited at last, like necessity, fortuity and the thief. The last temptation of Christ will not take place, there remains of catharsis but laughter, parody and imposture.

Beyond the narrative of the assorted dreams and desires of procreation, there also emerges from the shadows the story of King Herod as it is recalled by Jakub in a conversation with Bertlef. Herod's act of ordering the murder of every child when he learns that the future king of the Jews has just been born, is not, according to Jakub, an act of murder but one of total disagreement with humanity as created by the Lord. "I will destroy man whom I have created . . . for it repenteth me that I have made them," says Bertlef repeating Moses' words in chapter six of Genesis.[4] For Jakub, the terrible murder perpetrated by King Herod is not so much a crime against humanity as an act of generosity which seeks to deliver "the world from the clutches of mankind" (FP, p. 94). This novel about motherhood and fatherhood thus relentlessly confounds the last myths of our age, by marking them as so many comic elements. In fact, on the novelistic stage of constant procreative repetitions (of children and chairs, as Jacques would say to his master), people happily converse about the best way to rid humanity of people.

Back in Paradise . . .

The variations on procreation quietly restore, in a brilliant Kunderian paradox, several of his Don Juans to Paradise: his characters, with their desire to rid humanity of people, in fact end up with the dream of "not being a man," a theme which is even more pronounced in *The Unbearable Lightness of Being* than in *The Farewell Party*. Does Tomas, the great Don Juan of knowledge, not dream in his own way of being like Karenin or Adam in Paradise where man was not yet acquainted with excitement, with the result that his "nudity" as well as his sexuality only responded to the mechanics of procreation, at the first requirement of the categorical agreement with being?[5] Tomas agrees to a certain extent with Tereza's dream of an idyll, although his perspective is the reverse. Pondering the illness of her dog, Karenin, Tereza realizes that the idyll of "selfless love" is an anthropological impossibility, because man seems incapable of desiring the "simple presence" of the loved one. She is at this point not far removed from the new animal utopia of which her Don Juan of a husband starts to dream in his desire to dissociate love from "the aggressive stupidity of sex." For Tereza, in Paradise "Adam was like Karenin," the two being particularly alike in their lack of narcissism: Karenin does not recognize herself in her image quite simply because she is totally indifferent to it! The narrator extends the comparison, leading us more deeply than Tereza could have into his game of novelistic meditation: in Paradise, "man had not yet been cast out on man's path. Now we are longtime outcasts, flying through the emptiness of time in a straight line. . . . The longing for paradise is man's longing not to be man" (ULB, p. 296).

We are thus brought back, on the wings of nostalgia, to the problem of repetition since the desire of man not to be man is akin with that of the "happiness of repetition" which Tereza can experience with her dog, without ever experiencing it with Tomas. Because Karenin, unlike humans, was not driven out of Paradise and is therefore unaware of the duality of mind and body just as he is unaware of humanity's excitement and "disgust" in the face of filth. In this way Tereza discovers that the love which binds her to her dog is better than the one which exists between her and Tomas. "Better, not greater," emphasizes the narrator to avoid any hasty conclusions being drawn: it is not a quantitative, but a qualitative, difference. Kundera here evidently broaches one of the greatest paradoxes (as sad as it is laughable) of the human condition, a paradox which has its final variation in *Immortality*: disinterested love between humans was not foreseen by the Creator. The theme is ultimately developed through Agnes. Just like Tereza, Agnes strays from the very road of humanity precisely to escape from the faux pas of the Creator with whom she is in total disagreement—"how to live in a world with which one does not agree?" By imagining another life after death, Agnes knows that she would not want to meet Paul, her husband. At this point she decides, rather than to continue living a love based solely on the "will to love," to travel far away from all her nearest and dearest, far away from her husband and her daughter Brigitte. But to go where, to what refuge? Agnes knows that, to escape the "divine computer," people of old could seek refuge either in a convent, or in love. But she realized a long time ago that, in today's world, one cannot find refuge anywhere, in any "charter-house of Parma," and that there are also few people who know how to love or, in her own words, for whom in love "the other is more important than oneself," more important than "the divine computer" which claims to impart meaning to all things.

"Perhaps the reason we are unable to love," stated the narrator who followed Tereza's thoughts in the previous novel, "is that we yearn to be loved, that is, we demand something (love) from our partner instead of delivering ourselves up to him demand-free and asking for nothing but his company" (ULB, p. 297). The narrator of *Immortality* pursues the theme through Agnes' thoughts as much as through his own meditations on love which lead, in this last novel, to the questioning of the possibilities between love-emotion and love-relation. Close to Agnes's thoughts, love-relation rests for him on the knowledge between two people: it is an "inimitable, uninterchangeable love, destined for him who planted it, for him who is beloved, and therefore a non-transformable, non-transferable love" (IMM, p. 190). How can we not see in this kind of love a variation of his praise of erotic friendship in *The Unbearable Lightness of Being* or of the "beyond love" to which both Agnes and Rubens belong. Love-relation is thereby diametrically opposed to the "love-emotion" which Bettina von Arnim pompously terms "true love" (*wahre Liebe*) and whose origin has more to do with the divine than with people. Love-emotion "knows nothing of infidelity, for even when the object changes, the love itself remains perpetually the same flame lit by the same divine hand" (ibid.). We are a long way from Don Juan's journey knowledge, brought back "on the wings of enthusiasm" to paraphrase the narrator of *Immortality*, to the very heart of European love: towards homo sentimentalis.

For a Phenomenology of Love

Beyond the thematic ramifications which make up the unity of Kundera's work, beyond his questioning of time, memory, forgetting, history, laughter and kitsch, there emerges the theme of love as a central semantic and existential category. But what is love if we combine it indiscriminately with Tristan and Don Juan, with feeling and excitement, with body and soul? Is it heaviness or lightness, suffering or joy, stability or change? Does it belong to emotion, to ecstasy or to reason? It is a state or a revelation of time? It is fateful, crazy or fleeting? Does it belong to an idyll or to conflictual reality, to fidelity or betrayal? Is it on the side of tenderness or violence, of sincerity or imposture, of tragedy or comedy, of nostalgia or irony? These are as many questions which Kundera's variations, through his experimental selves, ask of love, from the first to last page of his novelistic score, as have asked, each in their own way, the greatest European novels. Kundera's work, especially *Immortality*, provides a real "phenomenological metaphor" of all the existential possibilities of European love by summoning, at the level of the variational structure, a large number of texts from European literature: Cervantes, Diderot, Goethe, Dostoyevsky and many others take part in this meeting of the "immortals."

Indeed, like an archeologist of "European love," Kundera has been able to make his meditations on the feeling of love coincide with the history of European civilization, itself based more on emotion than on reason. In this way he allows us to see the many possibilities and limits of our inner time and, simultaneously, those of the time of Europe. Whereas for Don Juan, "love" belongs to the pleasure of knowledge and, consequently, to the relativity of all emotion and desire, for homo sentimentalis on the other hand, love sets itself up as a supreme virtue, as abstract as it is absolute. In this absolute of love, emotion, suffering, and lyrical ecstasy take part together in what Kundera terms ironically "hypertrophy of the soul."

One can therefore understand why the figure of Don Juan takes on so much importance in the narrative framework of his novels: it takes part in the epic and ironic subversion which the variational esthetic imposes on sentimental lyricism (whether we term it kitsch or romantic). Between, on one hand, Don Juan and his incessant pursuit of the image of the other and, on the other, the narcissistic search for his own image by the sentimental lover, the phenomenological questioning of Kundera's variation sets down his metamorphoses and dissimilarities. It is as though Kundera wanted to signal forcefully that, when it comes to emotion, the absolute is definitely not human.

Did You Say "Love"?

With Kundera the very word "love" is invested with a large number of heterogeneous attitudes and realities. Far from separating its different meanings, the novelist examines their border zone which reveals, like the cutting edge of a blade between pleasure and sorrow, between body and soul, their impurity and contamination. From laughable loves to idyllic love, from the love of a man to the love for a dog, from procreative sexuality to eroticism without love, from love-emotion to love-relation, from love-passion to erotic friendship, from the love of Tristan to the eroticism of Don Juan or from athletic eroticism to its mystical phase, the novelist explores these innumerable situations like so many terms of a reality whose complexity is itself diminished by the single word "love." Indeed why give a single name to such different things? After all, cannot each feeling be experienced in different forms? This is the question which Ulrich in *The Man without Qualities* also asks himself in his diary. With Kundera, the same questioning marks the imaginary course of his characters as well as his own specifically novelistic meditation.

In *The Farewell Party*, for example, the word "love" for Ruzena takes on a different meaning with each of her partners. Associated with Frantisek who loves Ruzena, the word connotes boredom and the absence of all erotic perspective; associated with the trumpet player Klima who does not love her however, it becomes her "only passport to the future." But in both these cases, love remains linked to procreation and not to any kind of amorous or erotic passion. On the other hand, during the only night she spends with Bertlef, the word "love" is associated for Ruzena, you will recall, with a real miracle which frees her as much from the feeling of weight of her own existence as from the devilish link which ties her sexuality to procreation. But this miracle, surrounded by the bluish light of a cloud of death, is only a further illusion. This strange "erotic" scene serves as a point of convergence of all the "blue" motifs which mark this sombre farce on love and death through and through. And the death of Ruzena who, let us not forget, is pregnant, signals radically the negation of all reproductive activity which drives her hometown every bit as much as the interplay between the plot and the theme of this small masterpiece of mystification and the unbearably comic.

But let us take a look at the "love" of Ruzena's formidable rival, the beautiful Kamila. With her husband, the trumpet player Klima, she lives a mutual, idealized and inordinately great love, which shields her from any possibility of procreation as well as from "sexuality without love." Is this at last then love in the strongest sense? Nothing of the kind because for Kamila, the word "love" means neither a real feeling of love for her husband, nor erotic excitement as one might have expected. On her brief encounter with Jakub, she suddenly understands that her love for Klima is based only on the idea of her own obsessive jealousy and that it is enough that the idea on which her feeling rests should disappear for her love to vanish as if by magic.

Even a Don Juan of knowledge such as Tomas, in spite of his many erotic friendships, comes breathtakingly close to the examples mentioned. After all, does not this person, so lucid and apparently rational, fall in love in a single night with a woman he does not know, believing straightaway (after barely one night together!) that he could not outlive her were she to die!? He tells himself in vain that he is no doubt dealing with a hysterical reaction rather than love, but he will nevertheless, throughout his entire life, cling to the image of a child laid in the "bullrush basket that had been daubed with pitch." Is he not also won over more by the insidious feeling of compassion in the face of Tereza's suffering than by Tereza herself? "To assuage Tereza's sufferings, he married her" writes Kundera (ULB, p. 23). This awful phrase reveals Tomas' entire existential dilemma, caught up between his desire for women and the image of love made of suffering, an image which is infinitely magnified by his dreams of Tereza. All his life, Tomas will be blinded by the compassion nurtured in his dreams, just like a moth by the light of a bedside lamp, the image with which Kundera concludes the last scene in the life of Tomas and Tereza. In fact, by espousing Tereza's "suffering," Tomas makes the first gesture in the future renunciation of his episodic libertine life, and through this, the first step on the road to homo sentimentalis where love carries the weight of destiny.

I am thinking of Agnes who, like Kamila, Sabina or Rubens, undertakes the reverse journey of Tomas' when she understands that her love for Paul is based only on the will to love, on the will to keep going on the route of their common biography. Agnes knows that this "will," which has long been a substitute for desire, transforms even physical love between she and Paul into mere mechanical gestures from which love has gone without them even noticing. Is she really "beyond the border of love" as her sister Laura accuses? Without a doubt. But it is in fact in Agnes' "beyond love" that for her (and also for Rubens) the most authentic love is hidden because it is disinterested, a *sine qua non* condition of experiencing a real love-relation.

A Mirage of Timelessness

In Kundera's work the lyrical and "hypertrophied soul" of homo sentimentalis grants love the status of an absolute emotion which finds its true measure only in the absolute of death—another way of denying the finiteness of all things human. The kitsch view of love substitutes this illusion of timelessness for the duration of human life; this is which is most strongly stamped with Kundera's irony. Clinging to the threshold of adolescence and the disturbing relativity of the adult world, his lyrical heroes, in their extolling of love and death, find a compensatory defence, as reassuring as it is laughable, against life and its succession of doubts, uncertainties and disagreements.

It is as if, for them, "the seductiveness of kitsch" and the "seductiveness of love" were one and the same. Let us examine the "Colloquium" in *Laughable Loves*, for example, a narrative in which people talk about love and, following the gas poisoning of the nurse Elizabeth, also about death, since this straightforward accident is interpreted by the other protagonists as an act of suicide. We are borne aloft on the wings of the absolute of love and death which beat in unison in young Fleischman's breast. When he visits Elizabeth in hospital, and sits at her bedside holding a bouquet of roses and declaiming his "perhaps I do like you" in a sentimental voice, it is not love which makes his chest swell (for he is completely indifferent to Elizabeth), but those very same superimposed images of love and death merged into a single glorified value, turning the scene into a comic variation on the tragedy of Romeo and Juliet. Fleischman at this point feels the powerful and voluptuous surge of a soul fired by "splendid and invigorating death" with which he has been presented, or at least so he thinks as a perfect prototype of homo sentimentalis. But who can live otherwise than by sublimating a love as great as death? Consequently, as soon as she leaves hospital, Elizabeth will immediately be forgotten and Fleischman will be able to flit from one woman to another seeking new sensations, his soul forever elated by the false grandeur of a fragment of eternity.

Jaromil in *Life Is Elsewhere* becomes, from that point of view, a perfect variation on Fleischman, with poetic lyricism thrown in. Jaromil pushes to the limit the ineradicable human capacity to substitute the image of one's ideal for reality, to hide the unbearable image of one's own immaturity under a kitsch mask of beauty. Unlike the lucid Ludvik in *The Joke* who rebels against his own lyrical age—the era in which others are mere "walking mirrors in which he is amazed to find his own reflection" and no knowledge of the other, Jaromil, for his part, will never escape the trap of his "beautiful" illusions on the absolute value of love and death.

In order to escape litost in the face of his own erotic mediocrity, Jaromil, who can only hate words such as "girls" and "love," runs away from reality in the tale about Xavier who even leads a young girl to her death in order to live, at least in his dreams, a "love beyond the grave." Jaromil's pursuit of the absolute feeling of eternal love turns even sex into something fanciful and erotic language into mere cliches. The merging of love and kitsch is what allows me to hear, once again, beyond Kundera's laughter, that of Gombrowicz's *Ferdydurke* or that of Flaubert's *Madame Bovary*: the novel's laughter in the face of the imposture of all absolutes, that of love and that of youth, absolutes which are shared, in different eras, by Fleischman and Jaromil as well as Bettina von Arnim. They all belong to the same process of derealization which their view of love, based solely on reassuring and compensatory images of their own desires, is bound to entail.

Love is either absolute or it is not, declaims Jaromil dreaming (together with dozens of European poets) of a grandiose fiery death, while his devilish creator lets him die of a common chill, as ludicrous as it is insignificant. It is as though Kundera, with the very death of his "absolutely modern" poet, had responded to the desire of *Ferdydurke*'s narrator who, in order to rid himself of the immaturity into which he is plunged by his promiscuity with Zuta Lejeune, dreams of inoculating her with a nervous cold and, through her, "giving a cold to modernity." But meanwhile, Jaromil becomes an extoller of the beauty of absolute loves, a lyrical extoller who is all the more elated because, for want of genuine loves, his poetry offers the perfect release for the narcissistic feeling of his own "greatness."

As long as Jaromil remains walled up in the "house of the absolute of his poetry," his desire for a love as great as death is a matter of ridicule. Alas, it is quite another story when he ventures out onto the road of reality. In moments of love with his red-headed girlfriend, his demand for total love rapidly transforms his feeling into greater and greater cruelty where the absolute of death constantly lurks dangerously. And when he finally understands, during a stormy discussion with the redhead, the disparity between his ideal and reality, he does not hesitate to sacrifice the real girl to his ideals, by a "virile" act of denunciation to the police. When the soul hypertrophied by a feeling of the absolute begins to magnify, it hardly discerns the border between illusion and reality; it can only swallow up, in its own absolute resentment, all the relativity concealed by reality. Jaromil's hurt feelings of absolute love can therefore experience catharsis only in his cruel paroxysmal act, the very expression of the ecstasy of litost.

The Ecstasy of Litost

What is absolute love if not the illusory desire for identity between two people? As soon as that illusion is unmasked, love suddenly appears in its ridiculous aura and becomes a permanent source of the feeling of litost. It is a feeling of pathos which thrives, according to the narrator of *The Book of Laughter and Forgetting*, especially in the lyrical age of inexperience and immaturity. Litost functions like a "two-stroke en-gine" where an unhappy love affair is succeeded by a desire for revenge to make the other partner as miserable as oneself.

The student in *The Book of Laughter and Forgetting* experiments in his own way, in the company of illustrious lyrical poets, with the litost of lyrical lovers. His involuntarily chaste night with Christine, the wife of a country butcher, is based on a semantic misunderstand-ing as ridiculous as the one which takes place between Jaromil and the redhead. "No, please, no, she says. It would kill me," begs Christine when the student wants to make love to her. Whereas she is quite sim-ply afraid of becoming pregnant, he, blinded by his poetic illusions of infinite love, hears unexpected promise in her words. "She loved him so much it would kill her, she loved him to the point of being afraid to make love with him because if she were to make love with him, she would never be able to live without him and she would die of grief and desire" (BLF, p. 202). His happiness in the face of a love as great as death will only be equalled, when he finally realizes (too late, as always with Kundera!) his misunderstanding over Christine's supposed "chastity," in an immeasurable litost of a lost opportunity. Stendhal was quite right to term chastity "a very comic virtue." The *litost* which the student feels in the "drab light of morning" brings him very close to the poet nicknamed Lermontov whose "terrible litost that comes from hypercelibacy" makes him hate all happy lovers. Kundera's demystifying laughter in all his variations on laughable loves as great as death has the added effect of destroying the received ideas with which we are deluded by all discourses that persist in creating a much too hasty and tragic equation between Eros and Thanatos.

In his playful meditation on the "theory of litost," the narrator once more jumbles together the private time of love and the time of history, that of Bohemia in this case. He refers to the history of the country as that of litost par excellence because it was born of a succes-sion of its "glorious defeats." In love as in history, continues the nar-rator, a man possessed by litost in the wake of lost illusions on his own greatness "takes revenge through his own annihilation" because, where the absolute of litost reigns, there is no room for compromise. When, in 1968, the Russian tanks invaded Prague, Czechs wrote on walls: "We don't want compromise, we want victory!" It was not rea-son but the feeling of litost which was expressed in these words, speci-fies the narrator, because at the time there was absolutely no choice between victory and defeat, but of a choice among several types of defeat. The novelist's irony goes even further when he questions, beyond the time of private love where the kitsch of timelessness has no doubt always operated, the mechanisms of collective seduction. Thus, as far as the narrator of *The Book of Laughter and Forgetting* is concerned, although in love and life the feeling of litost is expressed more through an act of revenge (and Jaromil, the student of "Litost" as well as Laura or Bettina are obvious examples), in the great history of humanity, he gives it the name heroism.

The Eternal Flame of an "Amorous Fiction"

We have seen that any portrayal of kitsch is based on a specific relationship with human time which it denies and that, with Kundera, it is in fact in the portrayal of the lyrical emotion of love that the denial becomes obvious and comic at the same time, that it appears as ecstatic praise of the absolute present or as a nostalgic idealization of the past. Whereas homo sentimentalis establishes the feeling of love as a supreme value to the point of displacing the criteria of ethical judgement into the domain of the subjective, love for him is transformed into a virtue based above all on the idea of suffering which has become the value of values.

To pass love through the "great samovar of feeling" brings about, as the narrator of *Immortality* suggests, a separation between body and soul where even the sexes are dissolved to the benefit of the hypertrophied soul. For the novel's narrator, Cervantes' *Don Quixote* remains the best example of the process. In love with one Dulcinea whom he hardly knows but whom he transforms into a fanciful ideal, Don Quixote thinks he is experiencing "true love" where the real object of his desire hardly counts. Similar in this respect to Bettina von Arnim and her "love" for Goethe, Don Quixote's feelings do not have "to be paid in return" either, since their object is not real-woman Dulcinea but rather *the* sentimental and eternal flame of love.

Feelings often well up, in each of us, unwillingly, writes Kundera in his "homo sentimentalis." On the other hand, as soon as we want to experience them (as Don Quixote decides to love Dulcinea, as Bettina "firmly resolves" to love Goethe eternally), feelings become "an imitation of feeling, a show of feeling" and love a mere pretence of love, which displaces homo sentimentalis into a corner, where he resembles homo hystericus. In his brilliant playful meditation, Kundera takes us once more to the kingdom of kitsch, where feelings, with their succession of tears and suffering offer only, to those who experience them, a narcissistic reflection of their own selves, ridding them in the process of all responsibility in the face of their most horrible crimes and acts. The peace of mind of homo sentimentalis does indeed belong to his celestial sublimation of all awareness of reality.

Suffering as a Method of Seduction

Love and suffering as the great European school of egocentricity, as an eternal and unchanging state, have no need of carnal intercourse. This is what Dostoyevsky exaggerates, according to the narrator of *Immortality*, in the framework of his love stories. Like Mychkin in *The Idiot*, Kundera's narrator is ironic about suffering, especially when it is directed at a woman's soul, and thus becomes an excellent method of seduction. Many variations on that seemingly innocuous little phrase "you have suffered a great deal" which Mychkin says to Nastassia Philippovna run through the great European love stories, from the princesse de Clèves to Goethe's Werner. By transforming love into passion, the idea of suffering quietly displaces sexuality into the pure and chaste kingdom of emotion and the heart.

> The concept of European love has its roots in extra-coital soil. The twentieth century, which boasts that it liberated morals and likes to laugh at romantic feelings, was not capable of filling the concept of love with any new content (this is one of its debacles), so that a young European who silently pronounces that great word to himself willy-nilly returns on the wings of enthusiasm to precisely the same point where Werther lived his great love for Lotte and where Dominique nearly fell off his horse. (IMM, p. 197)

It follows that the "true love," extolled by Bettina von Arnim and her defenders, emerges as the actual privileged uniform of our "absolutely modern" loves. It wreaks wonderful havoc with our illusions of being "revolutionaries" of love and sexuality.

Passion, compassion, suffering, jealousy, so many terms that reduce love to an abstract idea by often emptying it of any carnal meaning. The words "you have suffered a great deal" are enough to make us forget the "undress" of Kundera's Don Juans. I am thinking once more of Tomas, connected to Tereza by his finger and not his sexual organ, and whose nights are haunted by dreams of paradise lost, thereby shifting his donjuanesque journey imperceptibly towards forgetting and making him die—as Tristan.

From the Middle Ages to the era of imagology, from the sublimated loves of the troubadours to the comedy of modern seduction, nothing seems to have changed in the "kingdom of the heart": here, the love of suffering and the sufferings of love remain one and the same, with the result that love remains more a privileged domain of

suffering than of pleasure. In the kingdom of purity and "gentle ec-
stasies" filled with nostalgic reminiscences, Kundera's lyrical characters
are hard to tell apart from Emma Bovary: like her, they are captivated
by "the fantasmagorical appeal of sentimental realities" besides which
life with its succession of disagreements can only permanently seem
like an imperfect reflection. Enthusiasts of love-emotion are no longer
able to distinguish between real love relationships and relationships of
prefabricated ideas or images of love, between the sleepwalking artifi-
ciality of kitsch love and the disturbing complexity of a real relation-
ship.

Don Juan's Final Glance

Marked by its five erotic periods, the "dial" of Rubens' life becomes
the metaphor of all the paths which run through all Kundera's work,
paths both of writing and eroticism. But the dial, which is simultane-
ously erotic, astrological and scriptural, appears in the novel above all
as a "metaphor of life" and a "school of finiteness": the finiteness of
life in its appeal for desire whose beauty is now betrayed by time. In
the novel, even bodies are deserted by desire. They no longer do any-
thing but display, through endless series of images reflected by the
embellishing mirrors of their new temples, futile gestures of the
"desire for immortality." Their shimmering space invades the conclud-
ing scene of Kundera's seventh novel and becomes the ultimate sign of
the forgetting which strikes the subject even in his desire. No, desire
(the eros) has not taken refuge in memory,[6] quite the contrary: it is
also snatched up by its own image as if by a reduced two-way mirror.
Because, in the world of imagological ecstasy of *Immortality*, illusion
is stronger than passion, stronger than love, with the result that from
these we no longer desire reality but a spectacle.[7]

I follow Rubens' final glance, the last libertine glance which, in my
reading, merges with that of the novelist. Their common, clearsightedly
skeptical glance, is also haunted by the past, driven by a handful of mem-
ories, which, as we know, are not, with Kundera, a negation of forgetting
but rather one form of it. By writing Rubens' story, the author-narrator
seems to suggest that their common donjuanesque journey, erotic for one
and variational for the other, leads to a single utopia of memory. Where
there is no more memory of desire is where the narrative ends. The gram-
matical tense of Rubens' erotic imagination will no longer be the future,
but the past of which there remains to him, moreover, only seven fleeting
images, "as if memory (as well as forgetting) had since brought about a
radical revaluation of all values" (IMM, p. 315).

Beyond Rubens's donjuanesque discourse is outlined—as if in a double exposure—the journey of the novelist who has broadened the Proustian problem of personal memory "to the enigma of collective time, the time of Europe, Europe looking back on its own past, weighing up its history like an old man seeing his whole life in a single moment" (AN, p. 16). This is what Kundera writes regarding his own art of the novel. Rubens' glance does not do otherwise: far from restricting himself to his personal life, he casts his final glance at the memory of European eroticism, at the image of Agnes' dead face which haunts him as it also haunts the novelist's imagination. Rubens even asks himself whether his entire erotic journey has not in fact served only to make him relive this final image, "the only photo" remaining in his memory of all his past desires. "And now that photograph is in flames and the beautiful, immobile face is is twisting, shrinking, turning black and falling at last into ashes" (IMM, p. 328).

This is indeed the last image fixed in Rubens' erotic memory, the last thought of the novelist's imagination: paradoxically, it does not belong to a scene of sexual excitement, but rather to a face as a revelation of the very *essence* of eroticism. The fact is that Agnes' face merges, for Rubens as well as for the novelist, with the last image of shame to which they turn their last nostalgic glance. Agnes "concealed herself behind her image" to keep her private life secret and prevent eroticism from thereby losing all its meaning. She is like Sabina, who also knew, that "a man who loses his privacy loses everything" (ULB, p. 113). Indeed, it is shame, one of the key notions of the modern era in Kundera's semantics which, paradoxically, reveals his actual idea of eroticism. Developed in continuous counterpoint with that of nudity, the theme of shame with Kundera discloses eros as an opening onto the other, as the sole guarantee of its difference. In *Immortality*, shame no longer appears as an "invention of men," "their erotic dream." Rubens and the novelist know, for their part, that the border between shame and shamelessness, between the private and the public, has become unrecognizable. They know—hence their sorrowful shared nostalgia—that of their memory of desire there remains only, when all is said and done, a nostalgic desire for memory, that the end of shame (a violation of private life!) also signals the end of eroticism, and by the same token, the end of the modern era as the time par excellence of individualism and the novel.

Epilogue

A Lesson from Epicurus:
The Wisdom of *Slowness*

The essay you have just read was completed before the publication of *Slowness*, a novel which signals a break in Kundera's work through the change of language and form. Its publication afforded me the unexpected opportunity to avoid all the standard conclusions and to open my essay, by ending it, with another of Kundera's "voyages inside the time of Europe," with another formal possibility of his art of the novel. The acute awareness of form as a possibility of choice remains with Kundera a guarantee of such an "opening." For me, the refusal to give a definitive meaning to his novelistic score in seven movements, in short, the refusal to "conclude," amounts to not betraying the very essence of Kundera's esthetic, his fundamental ambiguity and his questioning. How can one conclude on a body of work one of whose main characteristics consists of disintegration, dismantling, and constant flashbacks and digressions, without misrepresenting its episodic, acausal and intrinsically incomplete nature? Hence, by way of an epilogue, the "wisdom of slowness," which is both a look back to the past and opening on to the work to come; Epicurean wisdom if ever there was, for it prolongs the wonderful pleasures of my reading.

The Meeting of Two Different Centuries

The pleasure we experience in reading *Slowness*, one of Kundera's most recent comic masterpieces and the first novel he has written in French, can be measured by the obvious pleasure taken by the author in making his longstanding wish come true: combining serious questions with lightness of form, writing "a novel . . . with not a single serious word in it." Kundera draws us into an improbable narrative feast in which meditation and mischievousness vie with each other, where the burlesque extravaganza of his strange "moonlit" midsummer night's dreams mingles characters from the eighteenth and twentieth centuries in a dazzling contrapuntal divertimento.

The note to the Epilogue is on p. 134.

Right from the incipit, the author-narrator determines the outward setting of the narrative: "We suddenly had the urge to spend the evening and night in a château," he begins, speaking of himself and his wife Vera who has become one of the characters of the novel. Nevertheless, any reader hoping for autobiographical confessions is soon disappointed! Right from the highway which leads the couple to the château, the narrator gives away the present where everything is nothing but "ecstasy speed" and dreams of the slow pleasures of days gone by. He invites us to visit the garden of Epicurus where a certain Madame de T. and her young chevalier, lovers for one inconsequential night, run the gamut of such pleasures. Madame de T. and her chevalier step magically out of a short story written in 1777 by Vivant Denon, *Point de Lendemain*,[1] a short story which for Kundera best represents "the art and spirit of the eighteenth century." Its dual function, the playful and critical, is revealed more clearly than ever in the building of a "bridge" across different historical periods. By combining short sequences on the eighteenth century with those of the twentieth throughout the novel, Kundera plays with a fragmentary composition which is free of any linear plot. By making discontinuity an overt principle of his composition, he also curtails any biographical referentiality of his numerous characters, be it himself or his wife, Vera, whether they are part of Vivant Denon's short story or the symposium of French entomologists which takes place in the conference room on the ground floor of the château. Kundera's inimitable humour springs from the interplay of contrasts between the eighteenth- and twentieth-century sequences. His definition of humour in *Testaments Betrayed* could hardly be more appropriate here: the intoxicating relativity of all things human; the strange pleasure that comes of the certainty that there is no certainty. Indeed, it is from such absolute relativity that melancholy laughter, in the manner of Epicurean wisdom, springs in the face of destiny, in the face of fleeting time.

In the Garden of Epicurus

Slowness, memory and pleasure (both earthly and spiritual pleasure) are not without consequence for the form of the novel itself: "There is a secret bond between slowness and memory, between speed and forgetting," wisdom established by the narrator as the first rule of "existential mathematics," which he had referred to earlier in *Immortality*, namely that the degree of slowness should be proportional to the intensity of memory, like that of speed to the intensity of forgetting. Consequently, when he reflects upon Madame de T.'s night of love in

Denon's short story, Kundera is not so much concerned with her carnal pleasures as with her art of conversation thanks to which Madame de T. imposes form on a period of time: she divides it "into different stages, each separate from the next" in order to "[give] the small span of time accorded them the semblance of a marvelous little architecture, of a form" (SLO, p. 38). The whole secret of the architectonics themselves of Kundera's short novel (also the novel of a single night!) is based on the lesson of Madame de T. who, as a worthy disciple of Epicurus, knows, as the novelist knows, that "imposing form on a period of time is what beauty demands, but so does memory. For what is formless cannot be grasped, or committed to memory" (SLO, p. 38).

Slowness is therefore also a real treasure of architectonics. Following the example of Madame de T.'s night which slows down her amorous journey as a narrative by dividing it into three stages, the novelist defers his pleasure—and ours—thanks to constant narrative digressions, interrupted moreover by two "interludes" which portray Vera's waking on two occasions (chapters twenty-six and forty-three). In fact, his wife's sleep is literally haunted by the "crazy imagination" of the novelist which transform their room into a "haunted château" in which Vera's dreams become "a wastebin where [he] tosses pages that are too stupid." There's no doubt about it, this happy mystifier is enjoying himself to the point of inventing warnings which his mother might have issued and of which Vera reminds him in vain in the middle of their novelistic night: "Milanku, stop making jokes. No one will understand you. You will offend everyone, and everyone will end up hating you" (SLO, p. 91). She need not worry! The agelasts who will find the novel frivolous and sacrilegious made up their minds a long time ago.

Dancers in a Comic Opera

The scenes of the different media "dancers" in the comedy of modern-day civilization, characters assembled for a symposium of entomologists, provoke one burst of laughter after another. In a really farcical production, the narrator mixes anecdotes, themes and characters who all imagine themselves to be living their moment of glory before invisible cameras and have no idea that they are actually appearing in an imagological pantomime: a certain Berck(!) is vying with Duberque for the best media image (imagological kitsch oblige); a journalist nicknamed Immaculata who becomes infatuated, twenty years too late, with the media image of Berck and who, wanting to commit suicide in the château's swimming pool, takes the time to put on the white robe of Ophelia of whom she is no longer anything but a ludicrous parody. The scene would not be complete without Immaculata's worshipper, her cameraman who is ready to follow her even in death like a pooch decked out in ludicrous pyjamas.

Also a part of the procession are Vincent, a young friend of the narrator, and Julie, a young typist whom Vincent is trying to pick up while fantasizing, as a great admirer of the eighteenth century and Sade, about her "asshole" which he transforms into a lyrical metaphor for the moon, the "asshole drilled into the sky." He does not know that his beautiful kitschifying metaphor, stamped with the heritage of nineteenth-century lyricism, in fact marks the negation of libertine obsessions. But the height of grotesque remains Vincent's simulated coitus with Julie. As though they were acting "for a sizeable, anonymous audience," Vincent begins to yell to the world at large that he wants to sodomize his lady friend of one night. "The penetration did not take place" declares the narrator laconically and immediately proceeds to question Vincent's member, which is "as small as a wilted wild strawberry" (SLO, p. 120), about the reasons for its smallness. And Vincent's member, anxious to justify its going limp (as though it wanted to get its own back on the ladies' "indiscreet jewels"), provides him with a splendidly rational reply.

How can we forget the Czech professor Cechoripsky, the guest of honour of the French entomologists, who had played a small part (despite himself!) in Czech history in 1968, at the time when it was briefly illuminated by "Sublime Planetary Historic News." Alone in the middle of this comic opera where his hosts have nothing to say to him except stupid nonsense (Berque, especially, stubbornly insists that Mickiewicz is a great Czech poet and that Budapest is the capital of the country), is as touching as he is laughable. The unknown discoverer of an extremely rare fly named *musca pragensis* (*sic*!), has his moment of glory—his "melancholy celebration"—during his short lyrical speech, before the image of his own emotion makes him forget the text of his scientific contribution. His triumph immediately turns into a laughable defeat, it disappears just like his "inverted circumflexes" (beautiful as butterflies) whose no less glorious history of Czech spelling (do you know Jan Hus?) marked his name until they disappeared in the French transcription. It is impossible to convey here the numerous comic sequences because the story of the novel is impossible to relate.

The Great Expected Infidelity

Whereas we recognize in *Slowness* the echo of a few semantic notes from Kundera's previous novels (path, speed, critique of imagology, nudity, memory, forgetting as well as love, libertinism, excitement, suffering, and pleasure), the structure of the novel, on the other hand, which is composed like a narrative mosaic of fifty-one short chapter-sequences, forms an obvious break with his "novelistic score in seven movements" that concludes with *Immortality*. The structure of the score, as we know, is based entirely on two form-archetypes defined from the very beginning in *The Art of the Novel*: "1. polyphonic composition that brings heterogeneous elements together within an architecture based on the number seven; 2. burlesque, homogeneous, theatrical composition that verges on the improbable" (p. 96), which is the case of *The Farewell Party*. This is the only one of Kundera's novels to be composed in five parts, and occurs—as I want to remind you—on the actual "fold" of the composition of the whole: three novels in seven movements; a burlesque in five; and then again three novels in seven movements.

Thus, in the name of such formal and semantic coherence in the score, one could assume the end of the novel cycle. Furthermore, Kundera himself has said he wants "to break out of my bigamy with those two forms," which had given structure to his novels to that point, and thereby move towards some "great unexpected infidelity" (AN, p.96). With *Slowness*, that step has been well and truly taken and with it, at least we hope, there begins another novel cycle. Novels to come? Certainly! But as the end of *Immortality* also suggested, Kundera's gaze will from now on remain turned towards the memory of the European past in order to slow down, for the duration of a novel, our devilish race to oblivion. Furthermore, it is the mnesic echoes—reminiscences of the novelist's reading as well as the semantic echoes of his own previous work—which drives the playful pleasure of *Slowness*, and which stamps the novel with Epicurean happiness.

Day breaks and the author-narrator, at the same time as Vincent and Madame de T.'s chevalier, prepares to leave the "haunted château" where all three have spent a fantastic night. The improbable encounter then takes place between the happy eighteenth-century lover and Vincent whose simulated performance has transformed acts of pleasure into ridiculous movements.

So, while Vincent takes off again on his motorbike at a speed which matches his desire to forget the past night, the chevalier, for his part, slows his step, already thrilled at the thought of his return to Paris, a journey whose slowness filled with gentle reminiscences will allow him "to stay as close as he can to the night," to safeguard the memory of his pleasures. As one might have expected, the novelist's final gaze rests on him:

No tomorrow.
No audience
I beg you, friend, be happy. I have the vague sense that on your capacity to be happy hangs our only hope.
The chaise has vanished into the mist and I start the car. (SLO, p.154)

Did Epicurus not say that it is enough to have been happy once to be happy always in one's memories?

Notes

Foreword

1 One would like to advise Eva Le Grand to examine, in another study, the case of Musil, who was also co-opted, intolerably, by philosophical discourse.

2 As Milan Kundera himself states in *Testaments Betrayed* (New York: Harper-Collins, 1995).

3 A theme developed in my own essay *L'âge d'or du roman* (Paris: Éditions Grasset, 1995).

4 I repeat here word for word Roger Vailland's analysis in his book *Laclos* (Paris: Seuil, 1953).

Part One: Kitsch and the Desire for Eternity

1 See in this connection Guy Scarpetta, *L'impureté* (Paris: Grasset, 1985) and *L'artifice* (Paris: Grasset, 1988)

2 Hermann Broch, *Connaissance et création littéraire* (Paris: Gallimard, 1956) and Milan Kundera, *The Art of the Novel* (New York: Harper and Row, 1988).

3 Milan Kundera, *The Unbearable Lightness of Being* (New York: Harper and Row, 1984).

4 It is Husserl who makes the distinction, in his logical reflections, between two fundamental anthropological attitudes. See also Petr Rezek, *Filosofie a politika kyce* [*Philosophy and politics of kitsch*] (Prague: Institut pro StredoEvropskou kulturu, Edice OIKUMENÉ, 1991).

5 From this point of view, Kundera's characters are closely related to the heroines in the novels of both Manuel Puig or Vargas Llosa (or to Cécile in Woody Allen's *The Purple Rose of Cairo*), and to Emma Bovary, whose affairs are nurtured more by her reading than by reality. I am tempted to speak of Jaromil's affairs as "Bovaryism in the masculine."

6 Scarpetta, *L'impureté*.

7 Friedrich Nietzsche, *The Antichrist* (London: Fisher Unwin, 1899).

8 The esthetic ideal of the agreement with the lyrical being of poetry was treated ironically in the very first story of *Laughable Loves* entitled *Sestricko mych sestricek* [*My sisters' little sister*] (Prague: Ceskoslovensky spisovatel, 1965), a non-existent tale in English as it was removed by the novelist himself from his completed work. I mention the text here only to emphasize the importance and continuity of the reflection on kitsch in the archeology of all Kundera's work, from the first to last page. The story very clearly contains the first of his variations on the *categorical agreement with being* of lyrical poetry, a theme which is largely reworked, as it happens, in *Life Is Elsewhere*. Furthermore, he had already made use of the scatological element as an ironic factor, insofar as in it he explores the passage from the fine line between free poetry which is allowed to imagine "God's posterior" to kitsch poetry whose imagery lets only clearly "hygienic" agreements be heard.

9 Umberto Eco, "La struttura del cattivo gusto," *Apocalittici e integrati* (Milan: Bompiani, 1982 1964).

10 Friedrich Nietzsche, *Twilight of the Idols* (London and New York: Penguin Books, 1990).

11 Tomas Kulka, "Kitsch," *The British Journal of Aesthetica*, 28, 1 (Winter 1988).

12 Jordan Elgrably, "Interview with Milan Kundera," *Salmagundi*, 73 (Winter 1987).

13 Jean-Michel Rabaté, *Beauté amère* (Seyssel: Éditions du Champ Vallon, 1986).

14 This imaginary conversation finds its *critical* variation, moreover, in "À la Recherche du Présent Perdu," part five of *Testaments Betrayed*, where Kundera dissects minutely, sentence by sentence, "a kitschifying interpretation" of a recent American biography of Hemingway.

15 Her act does not have the same meaning as that of Mirek in *The Book of Laughter and Forgetting*, who also wants to erase from "the photographs of his life" the woman whom he once loved and of whom he is now ashamed. For Mirek, similar in this respect to the Communist party which had erased Gottwald's image on official photographs, wants to destroy the images of his past precisely in order to be able to *rewrite* it, and thereby become—another grotesque illusion—"master of [his] future."

Part Two
Chapter One: A Voyage Inside the Time of Europe

1 Previously published in the review *L'infini*, 44 (Winter 1993): 73-97.

2 Roland Barthes, *S/Z* (Paris: Seuil, 1970), p. 12.

3 It is of some relevance in this regard to emphasize that *The Art of the Novel* takes up, like a variation, the title as well as the basic idea of a study in Czech published in Prague in 1960. However, while in that study, Kundera focuses his vision of the European novel on the art of the Czech novelist Vladislav Vancura, in the French collection of essays he deals with his own poetics: an interplay of echoes develops between the novels of Kundera, those of central Europe and, in the last analysis, the European novel as rethought by him.

4 Moreover, even if the essay *Testaments Betrayed*, unlike *The Art of the Novel*, does not explicitly devote any chapter to the art of the novel of Kundera himself, I am tempted to read it as his own "esthetic testament" which, as was the case with Stravinski or Beckett, attempts to prevent any betrayal of his own work. The fact that he incorporates himself as Kundera—author in the last part of *Immortality* which consists of the "celebration" of the end of the age of authors and their works, including his very own(!), seems to me to support such a reading. Let us also add to this the "author's note" which accompanies the recent Czech editions of Kundera's novels, in which he states that in future he will refuse permission to publish any text which is not part of what he considers to be his works to which belong the seven opuses of his novel cycle, the play *Jacques and His Master* and the essay *The Art of the Novel*. Obviously, the essay *Testaments Betrayed*, as well as his recent novel *Slowness* are henceforth part of the list. (Out of respect for these esthetic wishes of the novelist, I have not, with one exception, included in my analyses texts such as *Les propriétaires des clefs* (a play), three stories which he once wrote for *Laughable Loves*, his poems and so on).

5 *Immortality*, p. 299. The narrator of the novel recalls various gestures related to shame: Goethe's touching Bettina's bared breasts; Rubens' touching the breasts of Agnes, his lutanist; the gestures of Agnes, who, as she dances, hides her face or who, out of shame, closes her eyes at the moment of her father's death; or, in an explicitly intertextual register, the death of Miss Else in Schnitzler's short story which represents, for the narrator of *Immortality*, a time long ago where shame and shamelessness were still in equilibrium. Moreover, the theme of shame, closely interlinked with those of nudity, eroticism and peoples' gaze, runs through all Kundera's novels, from "The Hitchhiking Game" in *Laughable Loves* to "Souls and Body" in *The Unbearable Lightness of Being* where Tereza, just like the man whom Kundera evokes in *Testaments Betrayed*, rushes to close her window curtains when her mother ventures beyond the border of shame; this is in fact how, for Tereza, "the maternal universe" (the one where conversations among friends are shamelessly betrayed, just like Tereza's personal diary) becomes the synonym for a "concentration camp," in other words, for ubiquitous totalitarianism . . .

6 *Testaments Betrayed*, p. 55. In the first version published in *L'Infini*, 36 (Winter 1991), Kundera initially discusses only the metaphor of two periods in the history of the European novel, a metaphor which he develops in the book into that of the three periods in order to include the twentieth-century novel.

7 Ernesto Sabato, let us recall, has recourse to a similar technique in *The Angel of Darkness* (Paris, New York: Ballantine Books, 1991).

8 Milos Pohorsky, "Komika Kunderova Zertu," *Ceska literatura*, 17 (1969): 334-37.

9 There is hardly any European philosophical thought which has not been concerned with the problematic of repetition. The names of some of the greatest are: Plato, Aristotle, Kierkegaard, Hegel, Nietzsche, Marx, Bergson, Freud, Husserl, Heidegger, and Deleuze.

10 Glen Brand, "Kundera and the Dialectic of Repetition," *Cross Currents: A Yearbook of Central European Culture*, 6 (1987): 461-72. See also Gilles Deleuze, *Différence et Répétition* (Paris: Presses universitaires de France, 1972); and J. Hillis Miller, *Fiction and Repetition* (Cambridge: Harvard University Press, 1982).

11 Terry Eagleton, "Estrangement and Irony, " *Salmagundi*, 73 (Winter 1987): 25-32.

12 Friedrich Nietzsche, *Thus Spake Zarathustra* (New York: Gordon Press, 1974).

13 Thomas Mann, *Doctor Faustus* (London: Secker and Warburg, 1959).

14 The contrapuntal relationship between dreams and reality traces in addition a secret link among Kundera's various novels. So, for example, the dreams in which Tereza sees naked women awaiting death by the edge of a swimming pool can be read as oneiric counterpoints of the images of reality which Olga observed by the edge of a swimming pool in *The Farewell Party*.

15 Sabato, *The Angel of Darkness*, p. 364.

16 Robert Musil, *The Man without Qualities*, vol. 1 (New York: A.A. Knopf, 1995), p. 272.

17 In his postscript to *Life Is Elsewhere*, Folio (Paris: Gallimard, 1982), François Ricard says that, together with *Don Quixote* and *Madame Bovary*, Kundera's novel "is perhaps the severest work ever to have been written against poetry."

18 Vaclav Belohradsky, *Krize eschatologie neosobnosti* [*Eschatological Crisis of the Impersonal*] (London: Rozmluvy Press, 1983).
19 See in this regard an excellent article by Joanna Gromek entitled precisely "A Dog's Happiness"; J. Gromek, Szczescie psa," in *Kundera: Materialy z sympozjum* (Katowicach, 1986; London: Polonia, 1988), pp. 80-93.

Chapter Two: Novel-Variation or Crossroads

1   François Ricard uses the fine term "novel-path" in his postscript to *Immortality*, Folio (Paris: Gallimard, 1993), p. 509.
2   The film adaptation of *The Unbearable Lightness of Being* which reduces (kitschifies!) the novel to a linear story, with absolutely no polyphonic or multiple focus perspective (not to mention the substitution of the meditative aspect of the novel for Hollywood's decorative eroticizing), certainly had, as Susanna Roth, his translator into German suggests, a direct impact on the writing of the deliberately and experimentally "unadaptable" *Immortality*. See S. Roth, "MilanKundera a Kritika," *Promeny [Metamorphoses]*, New York: Czechoslovak Society of Arts and Sciences Inc., 28- 01-1991).
3   It is always possible, as one might imagine, to situate Kundera's novelistic esthetic in various literary contexts beginning with the national context, of Czech literature. But when we know that his variational journey builds a programmatic bridge over the different periods of the European novel's history, limiting his work to the context of a single literature, would be a real esthetic misinterpretation. The desire to remember the entire history of the novel, the art of variation clearly shows that, for Kundera, (as was the case with Musil, Gombrowicz or Kantor), there exists only "transnational"esthetic value. (Which does not in any way diminish the importance that any other given literary tradition or specific sociohistoric context may have in the genesis of a work of art and its literary value!)
4   Kundera himself lists a few of these series: body, soul, vertigo, weakness, idyll for Tereza, for example, lightness and weight for Tomas, the "misunderstood words" for Franz and Sabina. See *The Art of the Novel*, pp. 29-32.
5   The *hat*: this is one of the motifs whose variations run through all Kundera's work to signify the laughter which bursts out from the very border between memory and forgetting: I am thinking of the hat on Passer's grave (*BLF*) which provokes giggles in the solemn crowd during a burial service, or of Clementis' Russian fur hat in the same novel, the only thing remaining, like a ridiculous sign, on the photographs from which Clementis has been erased; but I am also thinking of the hat we encounter in *Immortality* at the meeting of Beethoven and Goethe with the empress as well as of the little nightcap which Goethe sports while laughing about his "immortality" to make fun of Bettina.
6   Even in the fascinating novels of Musil and Broch which provide an example of incomparable syntheses in the production of the first half of the twentieth century, the architectonic balance is not always successfully maintained. In Broch's *The Sleepwalkers*, for example, philosophical reflection sometimes stems from narration which is independent of the recounting of the story, so much so that certain chapters could, at a pinch, be excised without observable harm to the coherence of the narrative, through a process of simple juxtaposition, and would thereby obviously lose their hypothetical character of a specifi-

cally novelistic essay so characteristic of Kundera's novels.

7 This is what differentiates him, for example, from Musil's *The Man without Qualities* or Mann's *Doctor Faustus* where the reflection is attributed to the main hero. See Helena Koskova, "Kunderova poetika romanu," *Promeny* [*Metamorphoses*] (New York: Czechoslovak Society of Arts and Sciences Inc., 28-01-1991).

8 This section is a largely revised and expanded version of my article published in *L'infini*, 5 (1984) and entitled "L'esthétique de l a variation romanesque" (pp. 56-63). I have endeavoured to modify the text I wrote in 1984 especially as, by sheer chance, I found a complete plagiarism of it in the book in Polish by Mr. Jacek Illg, *W kregu powiesci Milana Kundery* ("Universitas," Studia Batoriana NR 2, Krakow, 1992; see the pages corresponding to my text 134-41), and, what is more, with no reference whatsoever to my article, with not so much as a bibliographical note. In this case, it is certainly not simply a matter of the "circulation of ideas,"but definitely one of "imitative repetition," because, I like to think that taking up a text word for word into another language, despite a "modest" change of "I" into "one," is not yet enough to turn an imitative repetition into a variation. Unless, of course, one thinks one is Pierre Ménard and wants to rewrite *Don Quixote* word for word in the hope of giving it an entirely different meaning. Does Kundera have any idea just how right he is, when he suggests that, here below, all is nothing but repetition?!

9 Broch and Musil are not the only ones to seek a new form for the novel. Ladislav Klima, a Czech contemporary of Kafka, dreamt of a novelistic synthesis by recalling, as Kundera does today, Sterne's formal humour: "The form we have given the novel up until now is too narrow" Klima wrote in 1910. "The creation of a new and free form which allows itself everything and over which can be heard everywhere the mocking laughter of supreme and divine skepticism is only a question of time—Tristram Shandy to the nth power. As Wagner did for opera, so could the novel be recast in a universal literary form: it is a far more appropriate receptacle than a theoretical work including all the manifestations of spiritual life; in theoretical works there is less space for literary elements than there is in the novel for elements of theory"* (Ladislav Klima, *Ce qu'il y aura après la mort* [Paris: Éd. de la Différence, 1988], p. 314).

10 Guy Scarpetta, *L'impureté* (Paris: Grasset, 1985).

11 Witold Gombrowicz, *Ferdydurke,* translated by Eric Nosbacher (London: Macgibbon and Kee, 1961), p. 16.

12 Even death becomes a media event, served up to the cameras which track down people even as they are dying in front of everyone, transforming the world into an imagological version of an unimaginable panopticon. Everyone sees to it that the furthest reaches of private and personal life are made public and immortal. The "eleventh commandment" which Kundera adds to the decalogue replaces the right to ask questions by the "right to demand answers," thereby extending the imagological imperative to every form of communication: to the visual beauty mask is now added the "acoustic mask" of the media, to borrow, in a slightly different context, Elias Canetti's wonderful expression (on the subject of the acoustic mask in Canetti's work, see Suzanne Rothova, *Hlucna samota a horké stesti Bohumila Hrabala* [*The Noisy Solitude and Bitter Happiness of Bohumil Hrabal*] [Prague: Ed. Prazska imaginace, 1993], p. 105).

13 Jean Baudrillard, *Les stratégies fatales* (Paris: Grasset, 1983), p. 73.
14 Jan Patocka, *Qu'est-ce que la phénoménologie* (Grenoble: Éditions Jérôme Millon, 1988), p. 145.
15 Umberto Eco, *Sémiotique et philosophie du langage* (Paris: PUF, 1988).

Part Three: Don Juan's Final Glance, or the Memory of Desire

1 Milan Kundera, "American anti-kitsch," preface to Philip Roth, *Professeur du désir*, Folio (Paris: Gallimard, 1982).
2 Georges Bataille, *L'érotisme*, 10/18 (Paris: Union générale d'éditions, 1957), p. 189.
3 Ibid., p. 35.
4 The narrator of *The Unbearable Lightness of Being* is reflecting, from chapter one onwards, on what is clearly a variation in the negative on the first agreement with being.
5 The refusal by Kundera's libertines to procreate must be interpreted in contrast with this image of paradise, because, for them, the love between parent and child is an expression par excellence of a "required love" and one which is even totalitarian if one thinks of Jaromil and his mother! With such a required love, the narrator contrasts the disinterested and voluntary love of which Tereza dreams on the death of her dog.
6 I am alluding here to the book by Maria Nemcova Banerjee, *Paradoxes terminaux: Les romans de Milan Kundera* (Paris: Gallimard, 1993), p. 277, in which she writes, with regard to *Immortality*: "Exiled from reality, Eros takes refuge in memory: he demands a domain set above physical possibilities."*
7 See in this regard Jean Baudrillard, *Les stratégies fatales* (Paris: Grasset, 1983).

Epilogue: A Lesson from Epicurus: The Wisdom of *Slowness*

1 Vivant Denon, *Point de Lendemain* (Paris: Les Belles Lettres, 1993), p. 135.

Bibliography

Books on the Works of Milan Kundera

Aji, Aron, ed. *Milan Kundera and the Art of the Fiction* (a collection of critical essays). New York/London: Garland, 1992.

Brand, Glen. *Milan Kundera: An Annotated Bibliography*. New York, London: Garland, 1988.

Chvatik, Kvetoslav. *Die Fallen der Welt der Romancier Milan Kundera.* Munich, Vienna: Carl Hansen Verlag, 1994. *Le monde romanesque de Milan Kundera.* Trans. by B. Lortholary. Paris: Gallimard/Arcades, 1995.

Espejo, Miguel. *La ilusion lirica.* Buenos Aires: Hachette, 1984.

Fèvre, Fermin. *La espera verdad.* Buenos Aires: Editoriale Lexicus, 1987.

Illg, Jacek. *W kregu powiesci Milana Kundery.* "Universitas," Studia Batoriana NR 2: Krakow, 1992.

Misurella, Fred. *Understanding Milan Kundera, Public Events, Private Affairs.* Columbia: University of South Carolina Press, 1993.

Nemcova Banerjee, Maria. *Terminal Paradox: The Novels of Milan Kundera.* New York: Grove Weidenfeld, 1990; *Paradoxes terminaux.* Trans. by Nadia Akrouf. Paris: Gallimard, 1993.

Porter, Robert. *Kundera: A Voice from Central Europe.* Aarhus, Denmark: Arkona Press, 1981.

Issues of Journals and Proceedings of Symposia Devoted to the Works of Milan Kundera

Dialog, 6 (1986) (Symposium on Kundera); papers by Z. Ivankovic, D. Karahasan, Z. Konstantinovic, T. Kolenovic, P. Matvejevic, F. Muhic, J. Osti, I. Pandiz, J. Samic, V. Viskovic.

Europaische Ideen, Hf 20 (1976); articles by L. Aragon, P. Lainé, A. W. Mytze.

Hermes (March 1995); articles by Yoshinari Nishigana, Osamu Nishitani, Anna Hagino, Atuka Okada.

L'infini, 5 (1984); articles by E. Le Grand, S. Richterova.

L'Infini, 44 (Winter 1993); articles by Ph. Forest, E. Le Grand, L. Proguidis.

KUNDERA. Matterialy z sympozjum zorganizowageno w Katowicach w dniach 25-26 kwietnia 1986 r. London: Polonia, 1988; papers by J. Baluch, F. M. Cataluccio, E. Graczyk, J. Gromek, J. Illg, A. Jagodzinski, S. Kalinus, L. Kleberg, M. Leski, E. Morawiec, J. Olejniczak, D. Siwicka, K. Welt, M. Wyka, J. Zarek.

Liberté, 121 (1979); articles by N. Biron, F. Ricard.

Promeny, 28, 1 (1991); articles by J. Bayley, D. Gostynska, H. Koskova, P. Kussi, E. Le Grand, M. Nemcova Banerjee, F. Ricard, S. Roth, G. Scarpetta, Ph. Sollers, J. Toman.

Salmagundi, 73 (1987); articles by J. Bayley, C. Bedient, T. Molesworth, F. Ricard, G. Scarpetta.

The Review of Contemporary Fiction 9, 2 (summer 1989); articles by J. Bayley, A. S. Caldwell, Italo Calvino, K. Chvatik, M. Nemcova Banerjee, P. von Morstein, F. Ricard, I. Stavans, B. Very.

Other Essays on the Works of Milan Kundera (Abridged Bibliography)

Aragon, Louis. "Ce roman que je tiens pour une oeuvre majeure." In *La plaisanterie*. Paris: Gallimard, 1968.

Brodsky, Joseph. "Why Milan Kundera Is Wrong about Dostoyevsky." *New York Times Book Review*, February 17, 1985.

Dolezel, Lubomir. "Narrative Symposium in Milan Kundera's *The Joke*." *Narrative Modes in Czech Literature*. Toronto: University of Toronto Press, 1973.

Donahue, Bruce. "Laughter and Ironic Humor in the Fiction of Milan Kundera." *Critique: Studies in Modern Fiction*. Atlanta: n.p., 1984.

Eagle, Herbert. "Gender and Paradigm in Milan Kundera's *The Book of Laughter and Forgetting*." *Language and Literary Theory: In Honor of Ladislav Matejka*. Ann Arbor: University of Michigan Press, 1984.

Fuentes, Carlos. "The Other K." *Myself with Others*. New York: Farrar, Straus and Giroux, 1988.

Hersant, Yves. "Milan Kundera: la légère pesanteur du kitsch." *Critique*, no. 450.

Klima, Ivan. "Kunderova Nesmrtelnost." *Pritomnost*, c. 3.26, 1990.

Koskova, Helena. "Memento mori Evropy v proze Milana Kundery." *Hledani ztracené generace*. Toronto: Sixty-Eight Publishers, 1987.

Le Grand, Eva. "Milan Kundera, *auteur de Jacques le Fataliste*." *Stanford French Review*, 7, 2-3 (1984).

————. "La Liberté de l'imaginaire: *L'insoutenable légèreté de l'être*." *De la philosophie comme passion de la liberté*. Québec: Éditions du Beffroi, 1984.

————. "Kitsch, amour et séduction (Kundera, Puig et Vargas Llosa)." *Atelier du roman*, 3 (1994).

Lodge, David. "Milan Kundera, and the Idea of the Author in Modern Criticism." *After Bakhtin, Essays on Fictions and Criticism*. London: Routledge, 1990.

Mertens, Pierre. "Kundera ou le point de vue du roman." *L'agent double. Sur Duras, Gracq, Kundera, etc*. Bruxelles: Éditions Complexe, 1989.

Pochoda, Elizabeth. "Introduction." *Milan Kundera: The Farewell Party*. New York: Penguin Books, 1977.

Rabaté, Jean-Michel. "Le sourire du somnambule: de Broch à Kundera." *Critique*, 433-434 (June-July 1983).

Ricard, François. "Le point de vue de Satan"; "Variations sur l'art de la variation"; and "Des fleuves et d'un chien." In *La littérature contre elle-même*. Montreal: Boréal Express, 1985.

————. L'Idylle et l'idylle." Postscript to *L'insoutenable légèreté de l'être*. Folio. Paris: Gallimard, 1986.

_____. "Mortalité d'Agnès." postscript to *L'immortalité*. Folio. Paris: Gallimard, 1993.

_____. "Le recueil du collectionneur." postscript to *Risibles amours*. Folio. Paris: Gallimard, 1994.

Richterova, Sylvie. "Tri romany Milana Kundery." In *Slovo a ticho*. Munich: Edice Arkyr, 1986.

Roth, Philip. "Introducing Milan Kundera." In *Laughable Loves*. New York: Alfred A. Knopf, 1985.

Roy, Claude. "Jeu de massacre sur grandes figures." In *Le Nouvel Observateur*, Paris: 1973; also as postcript to *Zivot je jinde*. Toronto: Sixty-Eight Publishers, 1979.

Scarpetta, Guy. "Le quatuor de Kundera." In *L'impureté*. Paris: Grasset, 1985.

Sollers, Philippe. "Le diable mène la danse." *Le Nouvel Observateur* (Paris). November 1, 1990.

Updike, John. "Czech Angels." *Hugging the Shore: Essays and Criticism*. New York: Vintage, 1984.

www.ingramcontent.com/pod-product-compliance
Lightning Source LLC
Chambersburg PA
CBHW070612120726
47909CB00004B/1192